BODY UNDER THE CAFE

A VIKING WITCH MYSTERY

CATE MARTIN

Cover design by Shezaad Sudar.

Rune art by BettyStrange at Dreamstime.com.

Ratatoskr Press logo by Aidan Vincent Kise.

ISBN 978-1-958606-32-2

❀ Formatted with Vellum

CHAPTER ONE

IT WAS A GORGEOUS JUNE AFTERNOON, just three days until Midsummer, the date of Kara and Thorge's wedding. Everything was nearly ready, the entire village square all around the communal well festooned for the nuptials. The white-sided tents had been set up around the perimeter just that morning, their canvas flaps slapping in the soft breeze. The tables and benches were arranged in neat rows.

And everything, including me, was turned to face the floral bower that stood at the southern end of the square, its arch framing the view of the hills and meadows to the south of Villmark.

The sun was warm, but with puffy white clouds obscuring it for minutes at a time, it never got too hot. That should be a good thing, especially as I had been deep into my work before I realized I had forgotten to grab my sunhat. But the changing light was making my work a little more difficult than I had anticipated.

I may have overestimated how much I remembered from my oil painting class back in art school. I had never painted with oils before that class, and after passing my final and getting my grade, I had never done it again. I prefer the stark contrasts of pen and ink, or all the shades of gray I could evoke with charcoals.

But when I had decided to commemorate the lavish beauty of the floral bower that my friends would be exchanging vows under in just three days, I knew monochrome just wasn't going to cut it. I could've done a sketch with colored pencils. I had several very nice sets and knew some techniques to make the finished product glow beautifully.

But for some reason, oil painting had emerged from the depths of my memory and called out to me.

It might have been the sight of those flowers when they'd arrived. Not so much the clasping dogbane, which was pretty in a Queen Anne Lace sort of way, but those white flowers would've been very doable by my usual methods.

No, it was the Flodman's thistle, when Thorge finally found it. It's rare in our part of Minnesota, but not unheard of. Still, he had been away from Villmark for the better part of a week, not patrolling with his brothers as his duty as guardian of our settlement usually required, but hunting for enough of Kara's favorite flower to deck out the bower properly.

He had come through magnificently, the tall basket he had strapped to his back heaped full with bloom after bloom, each one with its cut end carefully wrapped in damp cloth to preserve it.

I knew my grandmother Nora had given him a flask of water with a little something semi-magical in it to help keep them all fresh, but she had pretended not to know what I was talking about when I tried asking her about it. Half a year I had spent learning magic at her knee, but she still kept secrets from me. It's not like keeping picked flowers fresh could possibly be dangerous magic.

Although, knowing my grandmother, what she was using to keep the flowers fresh had some other, graver purpose. Using something potentially dangerous to do something both off-label, as it were, but totally innocent was very on-brand for her.

At any rate, once I had seen the rich rose-to-purple color of the blooms on the Flodman's thistles, I knew I had to work in color. And if I were going to work in color, I might as well go all in.

So there I was, alone in the center of the village square with my cat Mjolner sleeping curled up against my ankle, dabbing away at the canvas with the oil paints that Loke had found for me. His ability to acquire anything at all with no notice is probably best not explored too deeply.

Sure, he can travel through doorways in a very unconventional way, stepping in one door and then stepping out another that could be anywhere in our world or in several others. But those journeys were never planned on his part, neither the destination nor the timing. And given how often he turned up not dressed for the weather, I doubted he found himself with local currency in his pockets often either.

Yes, definitely better just to take what he gave me with my warmest thanks and not ask too many questions.

I was pretty sure the paints were from somewhere in the mundane world, anyway. Probably not Runde, the fishing village on the shore of Lake Superior that was Villmark's sister village just on the other side of the magic barrier that kept Villmark hidden from the rest of the world. Runde didn't even have a fully stocked grocery store, let alone an art supply store.

But they were in tubes with UPC codes and invitations to visit their manufacturer's website, so I guessed he had probably gotten them in Grand Marais or maybe Duluth.

Also, they had the smell of linseed oil, always a clean smell to my nose, although some people don't like it. Having smelled older, more toxic oil-based paints in my day, the aroma of linseed oil was quite pleasant, really.

Something less benevolent had gotten on the handles of my brushes, though. I wasn't sure exactly what it was, but they had felt vaguely sticky when I had finally found the box where I had put them all after that class in art school. I had cleaned them up a bit, but being anxious to get started while the sun was out, I hadn't done as thorough of a job as I probably should have.

I realized that again every time I wanted to adjust the canvas or move my paints around, because I kept unthinkingly putting that brush between my teeth to free up my hands. And my tongue touched the wood grain and whatever was still stuck to that wood grain, and I regretted my hurry all over again.

Well, I was nearly done with the painting now. I would just have time to clean up before meeting my tutor in the Norse runes, Haraldr, at his house on the south end of town. Then I was off to Runde to help my grandmother with the spells that remained to be cast so that she could safely reopen her mead hall.

I wanted to stay to help her bring them down again when she closed up in the early hours of the morning. But that would mean getting home to Villmark very late indeed. And then in the morning checking the painting over for any last needed tweaks before I absolutely had to stop fussing with it or it would never be dry in time to be wrapped as my present to the wedding couple.

I had tried to push back starting work on the next rune with Haraldr until after the wedding. But since the rune I would be bonding with next was literally the rune that signified marriage, he refused to budge.

And, to be honest, I was anxious myself to have a working knowledge of it before the nuptials started. That was the moment I would be closest to it, I was sure. Waiting until after the wedding to start working on it felt like a huge missed opportunity.

I had even less luck convincing my grandmother to hold back on opening the mead hall until after Midsummer. First off, her cabin in Runde was barely under construction and wouldn't be ready for her to actually live inside it until September or later. Probably later, since she was relying on builders from the nonmagical world. There was no way to speed up those contractors, especially if the fine weather broke. Which, of course, it would. Eventually.

But she had rented a mobile home and parked it in the lot in front of the Runde meeting hall, the decidedly dingy-looking building that was meeting space, post office, general store and local drinking establishment all rolled into one.

I hadn't seen her temporary home yet, but I had strong reservations that it would be homey enough to fuel her magic. Her cabin had been a truly magical space, in every sense of the word. The beams of honey-colored wood that formed its skeleton all sporting hand-carved designs that had enchanted me as a child. The flagstone floors of iron-gray covered here and there by rugs in a Scandinavian style.

The view of the river just beyond the herb garden she had kept behind the kitchen.

It was my fault it was all gone now. Well, maybe that wasn't entirely fair. I had been drugged by the murderous Mandy Carlsen, and if I hadn't used all my meager magical abilities to fight her, she would've killed me, too.

But since it's not so much my *power* as my *control* which is meager, defending myself from a woman with a gun had somehow ended up with all of us inside a cabin-destroying freak tornado. So maybe I was right the first time. It was totally my fault.

I had learned a lot since then. But wildly losing control of what I was trying to do was still a problem. The last murder I had solved, I had thrown myself back to 1924 looking for clues without a real plan for how to get back, so... you know.

The sun dimmed slightly, then more profoundly as the wispy forefront of a cloud moved past the sun's place in the sky to make way for its chubbier middle section. And that chubby section stretched for quite a ways. But that was just fine. Looking over my canvas, I couldn't see anything left that I still wanted to fuss with. And when I'm creating something and not just sketching to invoke my magic, I'm a chronic tweaker.

But this felt done. And it hadn't turned out as badly as I had feared when I had first started mixing my paints and had experienced a horrid moment where I was sure I had forgotten everything I had ever known about color theory.

I let myself soak in that moment, feeling that accomplishment, that sense of completion.

But the cloud obscuring the sun was making the gentle breeze feel downright chilly, and—as I had lamented every time I had found myself with that brush clenched between my teeth—I hadn't brought any water. I was thirsty.

As if sensing that I was about to move, Mjolner lifted his head and blinked up at me with his yellow-green eyes. He yawned hugely, his long red tongue arcing back in on itself like the World Serpent, far too big for his mouth, surely. Then he closed his mouth and blinked again.

"You're coming with me to Runde, right?" I said to him as I gathered up my things and collapsed my travel stool.

He meowed at me almost testily, like it was a pointless question.

"Sorry. You know I get lonely when..." I broke off, not wanting to say the rest out loud. Not even to my cat. "I get lonely sometimes," I finished instead, lamely.

He gave me a hard look then got up, leading the way past the floral bower to the gate just a couple of doors down that led to our little house in town.

I had no reason to feel lonely, I reminded myself sternly. I saw people every day. I had seen Thorge and Kara both just that morning when I had made them promise not to go anywhere near the village commons that day. I had seen Loke just after seeing them, when he had brought me the art supplies he shouldn't have even known I needed. And I was about to see Haraldr at his house, then my grandmother at hers.

Then I would see practically everybody I knew as soon as the sun set and the mead hall once again opened for all of Runde and Villmark to mingle together under the cover of the spells that kept the simple fishing people of Runde from realizing they were drinking elbow-to-elbow with the last living vestiges of a Viking settlement no historian knew even existed on the shores of Lake Superior.

Practically everybody I knew. But not quite everybody.

Not Thorbjorn, or any of his brothers save Thorge. Not Frór, the older guardian who was something of a mentor to the five brothers we all called the Thors. With Thorge no longer out on patrol, it meant more work for the rest of them to keep Villmark safe from things that, like themselves, weren't technically supposed to be here in Northern Minnesota. Things that haunted the magical realms between the outskirts of Villmark to the mountains far to the north that marked the beginnings of Old Norway.

Everyone I met assured me that all the brothers would be there for the wedding. They wouldn't miss it. And everyone who said that to me completely believed it. All three members of the council, Haraldr, even my grandmother.

But my heart wouldn't quite hear it. As was always true when Thorbjorn was away, a part of me was unshakeably afraid that I would never see him again. It was a constant part of me, that fear.

Mjolner meowed at me, almost a yowl, impatient for me to hurry and open the gate for him. As if he couldn't leap over on his own.

As if he couldn't just walk through without leaping, for that matter. I knew he could walk through walls, even if I had never actually seen it happen.

"I'm coming," I said, tucking the collapsed stool under the arm that already held the basket of my painting supplies. Then I carefully picked up the canvas itself by the wooden frame and carried it home with me.

It had turned out better than I had expected. I had to hold on to that feeling. Because, in some small way, it held back that fear in my heart.

I would see Thorbjorn again in three days. Three days, maybe sooner. Then that fear would pass.

At least until the next time he left, anyway.

CHAPTER TWO

I'VE BEEN to Haraldr's house several times since moving to Villmark. Nearly all of my lessons with him have taken place in his expansive library, the finest in the village.

But I hadn't realized until Fulla had opened that door down the end of the long corridor that ran like a spine through the length of Haraldr's home that I had never been there in the late afternoon. Only in the morning or at lunchtime.

I wouldn't have thought that it would make much of a difference. There was a lot of natural light in the room, but it was all diffuse, from narrow windows set high up, close to the vaulted ceiling that protected all the books from damage from the sun, while still filling the space with warm light.

But the pattern of shadows was different now than I was used to. I lingered in the doorway, my gaze sweeping the room as I caught all the little differences. The desk he seldom used at the far end of the room was in darkness now. The long reading table where he would spread out books from time to time when he had fallen down some research rabbit hole or other was currently bare, but the wood glowed in the yellowish-orange tones from a single shaft of afternoon light that struck it dead center like a spotlight.

"I'm over here, Ingrid," Haraldr said with amusement in his voice. Probably because where he was sitting, in a chair pulled close to the fireplace, was where he usually was when I called on him.

"Sorry," I said, shaking myself back to life, then rushing to sit in the chair opposite his. Despite the warmth of the day, a fire was crackling in that fireplace. Applewood, from the smell of it. Probably a gift from the women who tended the public garden just across the street from his front door. They had an orchard there. It was too late in the season for the blossoms to scent the air, and far too early for the fruit themselves to be more than hard little knots hidden among the leaves.

But the smell from the fire was smokey and appley at once. It lacked only cinnamon and caramelized sugar to complete the olfactory allusion to baking apples.

That was probably just the hunger talking. I had slammed down three glasses of water after cleaning up from the painting, but there hadn't been enough time to grab any food. Not even an apple I could've slipped into my pocket.

I was really bad at remembering to do the shopping. It was a pity Loke hadn't thought of it when he'd gotten me all the paints.

"Are you feeling cold?" I asked Haraldr after dragging my mind back to the present moment.

"Not particularly, but a fire always cheers me," he said.

As if I couldn't see the woolen throw he had tucked carefully around his legs. It was hardly surprising if he *did* feel cold. He had very little fat on his bony body, and even less hair covering his bare scalp. As close as we were to Lake Superior, the wind almost always had a chilly bite to it. You didn't have to be old and frail to shiver at its touch.

"I know a little about this rune already, so that should help speed us along," I said.

"In a hurry to get down to Runde?" he asked. He was a master at controlling his tone. So carefully neutral, and yet I couldn't quite say that he was intentionally being careful to remain neutral.

Only, as a member of the council of three that oversaw the village of Villmark, I knew that being neutral on the subject of my grand-mother and her mead hall was flat-out impossible for him.

"I promised my grandmother to help with the spells," I said, raising my chin a little. "She's ready. I promise you. I'm just there for moral support."

"She needs your magic if she's not pulling from Loke anymore," he said, and it was all I could do not to gasp out loud.

"You knew about that?" I asked.

He tipped his head to one side and made a gesture that was where a shrug, a nod and a shake of the head would meet. All those messages at once.

And yet I understood what he meant. He had guessed, and I had just confirmed it for him.

I chewed at my lip, trying to decide if this had been one of my grandmother's actual secrets, or one of the many things that she wasn't exactly hiding, just not sharing details with anybody.

I was pretty sure it was the latter.

"Loke hasn't talked to her about it yet, so far as I know," I said at last. Loke didn't like to talk about his own brand of chaotic magic at all. I knew it was nothing like what my grandmother and I did, but beyond that, I only had a few very sketchy ideas. And I didn't think even my grandmother had a clearer picture.

"But now that he's aware, she will no longer be able to use him as a power source without his consent."

Again that master of tone. It was a Schrodinger sentence. If I wanted it to be a question, it was. But if I thought it was a statement, then *that*'s what it was.

"She didn't need him before my mother left, and I'm here now, so she won't need him currently either," I said.

"So she needs you for more than… moral support," he said, raising an eyebrow at me in amusement.

"Fine. You're right. But it's still perfectly safe, I promise you," I said. "I'm so much stronger now, and so is she. If a problem does arise, we're both aware enough to find it and confront it."

"Yes, that's what Valki, Brigida and I have agreed," he said, clapping his hands together if that were the end of the conversation.

It wasn't remotely the end of the conversation.

"The council of three discussed this? Without my grandmother or me there in attendance?" I asked, just holding my frustration in check.

"That is our job," he said. "The important thing for you is that you have our approval."

I opened and shut my mouth several times before stopping in the mouth-shut position.

The last thing my grandmother needed, at least in her own mind, was approval from the council. She had made it very clear to me that opening her mead hall to the public again was what she was going to do, no matter what they thought.

But their approval was still a good thing.

Wasn't it?

Or was accepting that approval also telling them that their approval mattered?

Did it matter?

"You said you were familiar with gipt already," Haraldr said, his voice reaching my ears easily enough, but taking far longer to penetrate to my brain.

"Huh?" I said, shutting down my internal arguments for the moment. It was annoying since I hadn't come to any kind of conclusion about the council and their relationship to my grandmother and me as volvas, the Villmarker word for a witch who serves the community. But I wasn't likely to come to one in that moment, anyway. Better to leave it for a longer ponder later.

"The seventh rune," he prompted me.

"Oh, yes," I said, then felt myself grinning. "So appropriate for a Midsummer wedding, don't you think?"

"A wedding is one of its meanings, indeed," he agreed. "What else do you know about it?"

"It looks like an X, and is the reason why someone would draw Xs for kisses at the end of a letter," I said. "Kisses seal unions. Like marriages."

"I'm glad you feel so confident with this one," Haraldr said. But this time, he made no effort to hide the darker undercurrents of his tone. Not that he was angry with me or anything. But something had him on edge.

"Why is that?" I asked suspiciously.

"Because of the other meanings. The, perhaps, older ones," he said. Then he gave me a hard stare. "The ones more closely associated with Odin."

My heart sank. As a volva, a Norse witch, repulsion should not be my first feeling when anyone said the name of the All-Father.

Especially since I was pretty sure I hadn't felt this way before meeting the man named Odd who, before he had tragically died, had heavily implied he was a living version of that god.

I knew he hadn't been.

Or, at least, I was pretty sure he hadn't been.

But he had definitely colored all my feelings for the god I had only considered rather remote before I had become a volva. I hadn't liked to draw him much, in truth. I preferred Freya with her cat-drawn carriage.

Or Thor.

Haraldr gave me an amused but confused look, and I realized I was blushing.

At least this time, when my thoughts had leapt to Thorbjorn without warning, it hadn't been motivated by that constant low-grade fear he might not return to me.

"How are Odin and the concept of marriage related?" I asked, sitting forward with my elbows on my knees, as if that would make covering my flaming cheeks with my hands look natural.

"It is like you said. Kisses seal unions," he said. At my puzzled look, he pressed on. "All relationships require sacrifice, yes? Two people sacrifice bits of themselves to create a union that is larger than the sum of its parts. That's a marriage."

"Okay," I said, but slowly. I still didn't see how Odin factored into any of this.

But Haraldr just held my gaze, the amusement back in his eyes as he waited for me to work it out on my own.

"Sacrifice," I said at last. "That's an Odin thing."

"You sound so grim," he said, eyes downright twinkling now. Like making me face what the All-Father really was amused him to no end.

"Isn't it? Sacrifice is always grim, isn't it?" I asked.

"Your modern ideas are probably tripping you up here," he said at last. "You know what sacrifice means to Odin."

That had been another prompt. But at least it was an easy one. "He sacrificed himself to himself, to gain knowledge." I took a deep breath and summoned up more details from the wisps of my memory. "He hung himself from the World Tree for nine days and nine nights, and in return, he received all the lore of the runes."

"Leaving an easier path for you and anyone else who seeks that knowledge," Haraldr said.

"Thanks, Odin," I said with a sigh.

"Sacrifice to Odin is not a payment of any kind," Haraldr went on. "It's not one person giving up and another person or god taking. It's more like a marriage. The sacrifice creates the bonds that join us together. Human to human, or hero to god. What binds us together is loyalty and love. And that is what gipt represents."

"This is going to be trickier than I thought," I admitted. "I thought with the wedding and all, it would be a piece of cake."

"Odin is a block for you, as I've learned during our time together," Haraldr said. "But not, I think, an insurmountable one. In fact, from what I've heard you say about how art informs your magic and the other way around, I think this will be... how did you say it? A piece of cake?"

I chuckled at his carefully formal version of the slang. But then I had to shrug. "What's the connection between my art and magic and gipt, then?"

"Gipt represents the magical force that existed even before the worlds were divided in the Ginnungagap. It is the entire concept of giving all at once. Giver, givee, the thing that is given, the thing it is given to. All at once, undifferentiated."

"Okay," I said slowly, lost again.

But he just smiled. "It flows, given and received, over and over. But each time its transformed just a little. It goes back to the source altered from how it left it. Then it cycles again."

We sat in silence for what felt like forever, but was probably only a few minutes. Still, there were a lot of cracks and snaps of that rustling fire before I finally spoke again.

"I've been wracking my brain about what I ever said about my art that sounded like that," I admitted.

"And yet?" he said with a knowing smile.

"And yet, that *is* what it feels like," I said, not quite returning his smile. "Especially with my magic. I put something out into the world, and I get it back. But it's constantly evolving. Into what, I don't know. But neither my art nor my magic ever stays the same."

"I think that is the perfect place for our lesson to end and your practice to begin," he said. "I suddenly find myself craving apple cake. Funny."

Clearly, that was partly because of our conversation and partly because of the smell from his fire, but all I said was, "I'll tell Fulla to see if she can rustle up some for you."

"That *would* be lovely," he said with a wistful sigh. "Apple cake at Midsummer. When I was a boy, such a thing would be far more magical than your grandmother's mead hall."

I doubted that was strictly true. Villmark provided for itself as well as it could with its own farms, orchards, herds and hunting. But outside trade had always been a necessary supplement. Originally, this had been with the local Ojibwe, but in more recent times it was mainly through the people of Runde. The circumstances that brought apples into Villmark even in June were perfectly mundane: they brought them into the village, through the protective magical barrier, from local produce suppliers.

On the other hand, maybe it *was* more magical. I would rather spin the spells that kept the mead hall a safely hidden space than try to work out the supply chain to secretly provide the thousands of people of Villmark with fresh food year-round without anyone in the modern world getting suspicious as to where it was all going.

It was a good thing I was a volva and not a member of the council, then. I could play to my strengths.

I poked my head into the kitchen to tell Haraldr's helper Fulla about the apple cake craving. Then I headed out the door, totally unsurprised to find Mjolner waiting atop one of the fence posts that marked the boundaries of the public garden.

Then the two of us walked together down to Runde.

CHAPTER THREE

THE LAST TIME I had been to Runde, it had been February. Everything had been under thick layers of snow that had muted the outlines of the evergreen trees that predominated the area, covered the rolling hillsides in gleaming white, but up close the roads had been a horror show of mud, road salt, and gray slush.

That was all gone now. I had missed all of spring.

That was never my favorite season, though. Now everything was lushly green, and wildflowers were in bloom to add a spattering of other colors. As I followed the path from the cave behind the waterfall alongside the river down to Runde proper, I listened to the song of the water over the rocks beside me and the birds calling to each other all around me. It was lovely, almost loud enough to drown out the sounds of trucks passing over the highway bridge that passed over Runde.

I reached the back patio of the meeting hall and saw that in addition to rebuilding her cabin, my grandmother had also called in contractors to make a few repairs to the meeting hall itself. The concrete of the back patio had been badly cracked, the bricks that formed the fire pits missing in places, the shrubbery growing too close to the outdoor tables. Now everything was patched up, pruned back, or outright replaced where needed.

It had even been swept recently. There was a large pile off to one side of what we always called helicopters when I was a kid: the seeds from the maple trees that clustered behind the meeting hall closer to the bluff than the river. A few had fallen since the rest of the patio had been swept, but not many.

I followed a path around the building, still examining the exterior as I walked. No one had touched the aluminum siding. There was probably no way to spruce that up without replacing all of it. But the gutters were clean, the few places I knew where they hadn't been flush against each other and had left dripping gaps fixed, and the trim had been painted a subdued shade of blue.

But the parking lot was a mess of potholes, the same as always. And at the far end, closest to the road where the potholes were the worst, was my grandmother's rented mobile home.

And my heart instantly sank.

I had hoped she would follow my suggestion and look into the tiny house trend. She didn't need much space, but she did need something that felt like it had been crafted by actual humans who loved other humans and wanted to house them with love and care, if at maximum efficiency.

This was the opposite of that.

This was a box with windows so small and badly positioned they barely deserved to be called windows.

It was completely impersonal, its durable exterior painted some not-white color so bland it didn't even have a name.

And it was sitting on blocks. Somehow, that felt like the ultimate insult. I knew it was only temporary, but did it have to scream that fact so loudly?

I sighed loudly, although there was no one there to hear it. My grandmother's magic was very much based on the state of her home, and this, despite its name, was no real home.

But there was nothing to be done about it now. It was where she had chosen to live until the work on her cabin was done.

I screwed up my nerve, plastered a pleasant smile on my face, and knocked on the world's flimsiest door.

"Come in!" my grandmother called from somewhere in the depths of the house.

As if that house had depths.

But I let myself in. I had one foot inside when the smell of waffles assaulted me, like a living thing that was going to wrestle me into submission. It was almost sunset, when had my grandmother made these waffles? And yet the crisp smell with its hints of vanilla and the promise of scads and scads of butter was simply overwhelming.

At least I wasn't craving out-of-season apples anymore.

Stepping inside the door put me in an undefined space between the living room nook at the front of the trailer and the kitchen just a little further back. I looked to the kitchen first, but there was no sign of waffles or even of my grandmother's waffle iron. Was I imagining it all?

Then I pushed thoughts of food out of my mind and took another, more thorough, look around.

The furniture was not my grandmother's style at all, and I guessed it had come with the mobile home when they'd parked it here. But the pillows and throws were all hers. Not just her style but her actual work, needlepoint and knitting and even weaving all on display.

She had lost everything when the rogue tornado had taken her cabin away. When had she had time to create all this? I had only left her alone in the cabin on the shore north of Villmark for a month.

Or two, I realized. All alone, with nothing but time on her hands.

Mjolner didn't seem bothered by any of it. He just brushed past me, found a sunny patch on the faded sofa under the window that spanned the front of the trailer, and curled up for yet another nap. I put my art bag down on the nearest chair. Even with all the painting equipment taken out of it, it was still pretty heavy.

Maybe I didn't need to carry so many sketchbooks and supplies with me everywhere I went. Only it always felt like I might. The wand tucked deep down in the bag's side pocket never felt as crucial to my magic as those books and drawing implements.

"Ingrid, there you are," my grandmother said as she emerged from the short hall behind the kitchen. I peeked behind her to see a miniature washer and dryer taking up most of the hallway space. An open door to the right led to a very confined bathroom. The only other door was at the end of the hall and was closed.

As a child, I had often wondered what my grandmother kept in her bedroom that I was never supposed to touch, or what she did in there that I was never supposed to see. When I had found out she was an actual practicing witch, that feeling had intensified by a thousand.

But now that I had a little magic to me as well, I realized there was nothing unusual going on. Just a perfectly ordinary desire for privacy. Since people in Runde and Villmark both were constantly coming and going through her other spaces, it wasn't that weird that she kept just one room as her own.

But I still was curious to see what was in it. More handmade textiles? Some of the art I had given her?

"Am I early?" I asked as she headed straight for the sink and the few dishes she had left soaking there. A bowl, a coffee mug, and a spoon. Nothing waffle-related at all.

My stomach grumbled loudly.

"No, you're not early," she said, but cocked an eyebrow at me to let me know she had heard my stomach, too. "I don't really have any snacks on hand in here. I've only just started using the kitchen rather than imposing on the neighbors."

I doubted very much if any of the neighbors would consider it an imposition, but I didn't say so. But my stomach grumbled again, so I was forced to say *something*. "It's a shame the store in the hall isn't open. You always had those organic granola bars I liked. The ones with berries *and* with chocolate." Most brands made you pick one or the other, but why?

"Oh, the store's open," she said as she dried her hands on her dishtowel. "I keep forgetting."

"Shouldn't you be over there, then?" I asked.

"Well, you'll be pleased to know I've hired a little extra help for the daytime hours," she said, her cheeks even coloring a little, like she was embarrassed to even admit she couldn't both draw the spells back down at two or three in the morning and then open the store again right on time at eight. Even if she was only her apparent age of somewhere in her seventies and not her actual age of something more like a hundred and twenty, that was a lot to do every single day without a break.

"That's fantastic," I said, but carefully not as enthused as I was feeling. She'd bristle up quick if it seemed like I didn't think she was perfectly capable of doing it all herself. "Who did you hire?"

"No one full-time, but I do have two people sharing the work on a part-time basis. Keith and Ralf Sorensen," she said, naming them harshly, almost with a vengeance.

"That's the two that went bear hunting after you told them to stay in town after Garrett Nelsen died," I said. That had been only a month into my time in Runde, but I had remembered her anger at their absconding themselves in the middle of a murder investigation. Neither of them had been remotely involved in the murder, but clearly she was still holding a grudge against the both of them for disobeying her. "So, how's that going?" I asked carefully.

"Keith is all right," she said grudgingly. "Well, Ralf isn't a problem either. But I prefer Keith."

"So they're just watching the shop during the day?" I asked.

"They don't pour the drinks," she said, as if that was a line few crossed. Well, if it was her signature mead we were talking about, the mead she brewed all by herself down in the hall's basement, that was a line few crossed. In my memory, I had only ever seen her be the one serving it in the hall.

"That probably doesn't come up much during the day," I said diplomatically.

"No, you're right," she said. "Mostly, it's the contractors who are making the repairs. I need someone else around besides just me to point them in the right direction. But Ralf is a restless spirit. Minding the till of a store with few customers is not his calling."

"That's true of most of us, isn't it?" I said.

"Yes, I suppose so. But I've given him a new assignment," she said.

"What's he doing?" I asked, a little unnerved by her slow grin.

"Delivering the mail," she said. "Even the packages. He's got that brand-new pickup truck, and he certainly knows everybody in town. Plus, it keeps him out of the hall for a good chunk of the day."

"You'll spoil everyone," I said. "If you don't intend to keep doing it, that is. Has anyone in Runde ever *not* had to pick up their own mail here?"

"Only in the sense that sometimes their neighbors pick it up with their own and drop it off for them," she said.

"Well, if Keith is manning the till, I think I'll liven up his day a little by going over there to buy something."

"I'll meet you there in a few minutes," she said as she retrieved her walking stick from behind the door. "I have to say a word to the head contractor over at the cabin before he heads home for the day."

"Right. How's the construction going?" I asked.

I watched as she mentally sorted through dozens of responses before landing on a rather unilluminating, "On time."

Then she was out the door so fast I lunged to follow her out onto the uneven surface of the parking lot. But she didn't look back as I spun to keep the flimsy door from banging shut behind me. It had no weight at all; it was like trying to control the motions of a wind-loving sheet of cardboard. And there was barely any breeze.

Once I heard it click and was sure it wasn't going to blow open again, I picked my way across the parking lot to the newly painted doors of the hall itself and went inside.

It was so strange being back in that space again. Even stranger now that it had been spruced up a bit, the water-damaged ceiling tiles replaced with shiningly white new ones, the chairs with their cracked plastic seats gone in favor of molded plastic ones that looked a little more durable.

Because, despite the new touches, it was still the most mundane of mundane spaces. People met here to discuss local ordinances, to hold bake sales for the high school band to get uniforms, to sit and nurse a beer under the flickering fluorescent lights in companionable silence beside a neighbor doing the same.

And yet, underneath all that, it was the most magical place I had ever been to. And only a month before, I had stood beside a bonfire that had been burning untended in a deep cave for over a thousand years.

"Hi, Keith," I said. I had expected to find myself interrupting a nap, but he was fully alert behind the counter, setting a novel aside as he stood up.

"Hey, Ingrid. Long time, no see," he said. "If you're here to see your grandmother, she usually comes in a little later. Closer to sunset."

My mind pounced on that information. She had indeed hired help during the day, which was a good thing.

But she had been coming here alone at night. When the mead hall wasn't open yet. And the only reason for that would be to work with the spells.

Without me.

I wasn't so sure that was a good thing.

"Actually, I was looking for those granola bars. The ones with the bear logo on them from that local company?" I realized I was making a completely unillustrative box gesture with my hands and shoved them into my pockets. Of course granola bars came in a box.

"The dark chocolate and berry ones?" he said. "We just got a bunch of them in today. They're just behind you, on that end cap."

That sounded easier to find than it turned out to be. The general store part of the meeting hall was small, only four rows of shelves, but everything imaginable was packed in there. Looking for one specific thing in that sea of packaging was a bit of a challenge.

We were still playing hotter and colder like a couple of bored kids when the double doors opened again and a shadowy figure paused in the doorway.

"Ingrid?" she said.

But it wasn't my grandmother. It was Kara.

"Kara! What are you doing here?" I asked. But in the same moment, I had finally found my quarry. I took the box to the counter, then dug through my pockets for the crumpled ten I knew was in there somewhere. I hadn't needed cash for months, but I knew I had grabbed some before leaving my house in Villmark.

"I'm here to help," she said, then stepped further inside. She was dressed for Runde in faded jeans and a loose-fitting T-shirt with some sort of fishing logo barely visible on the front. How long had she had *that* shirt?

She came up to where I was standing at the counter with Keith and gave him a brief smile. Even dressed as if her idea of the "help" she was here to give was with the construction work and not, in fact, magic, I could see that smile hit Keith hard enough to make him blink.

Kara, like her sister Nilda, looked like a living valkyrie. Tall, muscular, with flowing blond hair that looked gorgeous even pulled back in a sloppy bun like it was now. I could scarcely blame Keith for reacting like he did.

"She's getting married in three days," I told him.

He blinked again, coming out of the spell. "Congratulations," he told her, blushing, then hurriedly rang up my purchase.

"I can't wait," Kara said, but there was a gleam in her eye that had nothing to do with her upcoming nuptials.

Because my grandmother had asked her to help us with magic. And she could scarcely contain her excitement.

I was starting to feel it, too. But mine had an undercurrent of worry. Kara hadn't been in touch with her abilities that night, when all the spells that were woven through the mead hall had failed. She hadn't known what that looked like or felt like from a magical perspective.

But I did. And even as I gave her an answering grin, I couldn't quiet the worry that something might go wrong.

I might not know as much about magic as my grandmother did, but I knew that much.

Something could *always* go wrong.

CHAPTER FOUR

I HAD DONE the mead hall protection spells with my grandmother
many times, although it had been months since we'd done them last.
Still, there was a certain magical kind of muscle memory that just
kicked in the moment I felt the power building in my grandmother's
hands being passed off to me.

But Kara was there too, and that was a new element, having a
third. When I had been a novice, I had been all raw power but no real
awareness. Kara had those proportions flipped. She could feel how the
magic flowed between my grandmother and me in a way I hadn't been
able to perceive for so many frustrating weeks. And she understood
what she was seeing in a way that had eluded me for an equally frus-
tratingly long length of time.

But, at least in this first casting, she was almost more of a hinder-
ance than a help. She could take the power when my grandmother
passed some to her, but she added very little to it. And she fumbled
almost to the point of disrupting the flow before she could hand it
back again.

Not that it was a problem for any of the spells at all. As we worked,
I could tell that my grandmother had prepared for just such a situa-

tion. Asking Kara to come down hadn't been because she had wanted a third set of magical hands helping. She had wanted Kara there to mark the moment of the opening of the mead hall as the start of her formal education into the ways of a volva.

It was the best possible indication that my grandmother had all of her old confidence back. She didn't even want to wait a day to make sure we really had everything in hand before throwing in a few tougher moves that upped the difficulty.

Clearly, that confidence wasn't misplaced. We had all the spells in place well before sundown, even though it had taken longer than usual because we weren't recharging old spells but casting entirely new ones.

That time she had spent convalescing in the cabin on the lake shore north of Villmark had truly revitalized her.

"You made some changes," I said to her when we had finally stopped working the magic and could sit together at the bar where she served her signature brand of mead and wait for the customers to start coming in.

"Just a few tweaks," my grandmother said as she fussed at stacks of napkins and freshly folded towels behind her counter. "The original spells were decades old. They had been the best I could do originally, and after all that time were more magical patch than original spell-work, anyway. This was the perfect opportunity to bring things up a notch."

"Is it going to work any differently?" Kara asked. "I mean, I'm sure we still have to be careful around the Runde people so they don't know who we really are. But it feels safer in here somehow."

"Part of that is because you were part of the spellwork," my grandmother told her. "You understand what protects this place in a way you didn't before. Of course that would make it feel safer to you."

"But it feels safer to me, too," I said.

"Well, I did tweak the spells," my grandmother said with a careless shrug.

I didn't press the point. If she thought I was ready to know the specifics, she would've offered them by now. And if she didn't, which she clearly didn't, I wasn't going to be able to wheedle them out of her.

Although she did glance up from polishing the already sparkling glassware to give me a sharp look. Like she really thought I would've noticed what she had done.

This really wasn't the day I wanted to feel like a failure. The spells were up, and the painting drying in my home back in Villmark was some of my best work. Those two things were enough to buoy my spirits.

So I just pushed away from the bar and strolled through the empty hall. Being nearly Midsummer, the fireplaces were all cold and empty, but the warm glow of the lights above had a fire-like quality. It was a welcome change from the harsh fluorescent lighting of the Runde meeting hall that had existed here minutes before.

I ran my hand over the heavy wood of the long tables, scarred by decades of being pounded by the edges of mugs and cups and the occasional knife, but smooth to the touch otherwise, with no hint of the stickiness that was sure to come. The benches were pulled out just far enough to be inviting, as were the chairs at the smaller tables at the periphery of the room.

I had spent so many nights here with my friends before my duties in Villmark had called me away. But it wasn't a homecoming quite yet.

Not until those friends arrived.

When a door finally banged open, it wasn't on the Runde side of the building. It was on the Villmark side. And the first person through that door was Roarr Egilsen.

As was usual for him, he came in with his hands deep in the pockets of his jeans and his shoulders rounded forward, almost into a hunch. He was a big guy; that made it tough to be as invisible as he would like.

And I wouldn't exactly call him a friend, although he was someone who was very much tangled up in my life. But he wasn't exactly an enemy, either. He was just an ally, but the sort of ally where every time we met, I had to wrestle again with whether or not I could trust him.

He *had* saved my life. There was that.

But he had also been the prime suspect in the first murder I had investigated just days after coming up north from St. Paul the autumn before. He hadn't been guilty of that murder, but he hadn't been entirely innocent either. He had helped the murderess attempt to cover up the crime, even though the victim had been his own fiancée. How much of that had been because that murderess had been a wannabe sorceress with real power named Halldis, who was capable of something very close to mind control, was a question I had never been able to find a satisfactory answer to.

But he had been working hard ever since to earn back everyone's trust. That I couldn't deny.

Roarr stopped just inside the doorway, blinking as if the firelight inside were too much after the twilight outside.

Then someone edged her way past him and headed straight to Kara still sitting at my grandmother's bar. It was her sister, Nilda. Like Kara, she looked like a living valkyrie. And she, too, was wearing modern clothes, if not so much designed not to draw attention. Her hair was in its customary long, thick braid down her back, and her button-up shirt was nicer than any fishing T-shirt. She was dressed to enjoy the evening.

She gave me a wink of greeting in passing, but made a beeline to her sister. Wedding business, I would bet. I hoped there was some subtle way I could hang back from that conversation without seeming like I was avoiding being assigned any of the numerous tasks still to do before the nuptials commenced.

But I was totally trying to avoid being assigned any wedding tasks.

"It looks like it all went well," a voice said at my elbow and I turned to see Loke standing beside me. He was dressed as always in black from head to toe and didn't seem to have come from the direction of the Villmark door. Or the Runde door either. But then he had his own ways of getting around.

"Very smoothly," I said. "And as best as I can judge, it should be much less work maintaining these spells than it was the last bunch."

"Your mormor might not need to drain power out of me at all, then," he said, not quite joking.

"Not unless you need her to," I said. She might have been siphoning his power to use for the mead hall spells, but she had also been pulling from him because he couldn't handle all the power that he was generating all the time without any apparent means of control.

Not that he saw it that way. But in that moment, he just shrugged.

Then the Runde door finally opened and a group of Sorensens came in. Better than half of the town had the last name Sorensen, although they divided themselves into two distinct groups based on their chosen vocations. Judging by their caps and footwear, I knew these were fishing Sorensens and not the farming variety. They weren't talking with each other, weren't distracted by their phones or anything else at all. And yet when they found themselves inside a Viking-era hall that smelled of mead and wood smoke, not a one of them did a double take.

The spells were working. As much as I had known that from working the magic, it was a relief to see it confirmed all the same.

Then a group of farming Sorensens came in behind the fishing Sorensens, and then more Villmarkers came in through their door at the back. That group was a mixed bunch, some dressed in modern dress as my friends tended to do when they came down from the village, but others still dressed in their conventional Villmarker clothes. These weren't exactly like what our ancestors wore, but they weren't modern clothes either. It was fashion from an alternate timeline, different enough to draw attention.

If the spells hadn't been working. But they were.

Then the Runde door opened again, and this time I did run over to greet the arrivals, Michelle and Jessica, with Loke still at my elbow. It almost completed the tableau of the first people I had met after driving into a tree at the crossroads where Runde met the highway.

Almost.

"It's so good to see you!" Michelle said as she pulled me into a tight hug. Her honey-blonde hair was still pulled up into a ponytail, and I guessed she had come here straight after ending her shift at the restaurant on that crossroads. But when she stepped back from her hug, there was a flash of something in her blue eyes. Just a hint of trepidation that was gone the instant Jessica pushed past her to give me a hug of her own.

"It's been too long," I said as Jessica gave me a quick squeeze then stepped back. Her light blonde hair was uncharacteristically loose, not in its usual elaborate crown braid. It was a small change, and yet it seemed to alter her entire appearance. Her cheeks were rosier, her blue eyes brighter, her skin glowing.

"You look good," I blurted out, and she flushed and nervously brushed her hair back with her hand.

"Thanks," she said.

Then someone else was suddenly standing behind her, and it was like I was seeing double. Same loose light blonde hair, same brand of jeans, almost identical blue blouses with a simple gold pendant hanging on a chain just where the fabric met in a V. I was pretty sure they were even wearing the same light fragrance.

Then she looked up at me and I saw her eyes were even more intensely blue than Jessica's. The color of the blouse matched Jessica's eyes really well, but it looked a little more washed-out on this new woman. I had never seen eyes so blue.

Belatedly, I realized all my staring was making her more than a little self-conscious. She moved half a step to stand a little bit more behind Jessica, as if for protection.

"Hello?" I said uncertainly. I had never seen this young woman before, but I didn't quite know everyone in Runde by sight yet. Maybe it was just a coincidence, how much she looked like Jessica.

But that faint hope was dashed when Jessica pulled the stranger forward until she was right before me. "Ingrid, this is Heather Peterson. Heather, this is Ingrid Torfa."

"Ingrid, of course," Heather said. "Jessica has told me so much about you."

"I wish I could say the same, but I *have* been away a lot," I admitted.

"Heather has been helping out at the café," Jessica said. "We'll get you all caught up in a jiffy, I'm sure. But let's grab a table first, okay?"

"Drinks, then a table," Michelle amended and shot me a conspiratorial wink.

"I'll have a beer," Heather said, looking around for any sign of a server. But of course there was none. My grandmother's mead hall was entirely self-serve for anything besides her mead.

"While they definitely have beer here, since it's your first time, you have to try the mead," Michelle told her. "Nonnegotiable."

Heather gave Jessica a questioning look, but Jessica gave her a solemn nod.

"Meads all around, and then a table," I declared, and headed to the bar to fetch the mead.

But even as I did so, I mused on this new person in my life. Heather must be truly exceptional, to be having such a profound effect on Jessica. I reminded myself that the strange magical women I knew who lived far to the north of Villmark had no way of reaching Runde. Although they had great powers of seduction and lured acolytes into dressing and behaving as the rest of them did, this couldn't be that. It had to be a more innocent moment of one young woman just really wishing she was more like another, more exciting one.

I hoped, anyway. Glamor magic would trigger the mead hall's defenses, so I knew this Heather person wasn't doing anything like that. But just mundane influencing on another person's mind could be problematic. I had seen it before, back in St. Paul.

And yet Michelle hadn't looked concerned. So perhaps my recent experience with the seductive, almost clone-like women was coloring my perceptions, giving me prejudices that weren't accurate on this side of that protective magic.

I would know by the end of a simple conversation, I was sure. And I was sure it was nothing that was part of my actual responsibility as a volva.

Still, as I waited in line for our share of the mead, I kept glancing up at the ceiling. At the spells I could see pulsing softly as they worked to protect all within.

There was no glamor here, I reminded myself. No magic. We were safe.

But that pulsing glow didn't quite manage to convince me. I was still edgy as I took the tray of drinks to the table the others had gathered around.

Whether this was magic or just a run-of-the-mill bad influence, I wasn't going to let anything hurt Jessica. Ever.

CHAPTER FIVE

MICHELLE, Jessica and Heather had gathered around one of the side tables in its own little alcove rather than taking seats at the long main tables. The smaller table was perfectly situated for watching the entire room and yet deep enough in the shadows to not be too noticeable to the others. And being inside a little alcove of half-walls, it was a better spot for the sort of catching-up conversation we had planned.

As I arrived with the mead, I saw Loke and Roarr were already there, although they had drinks of their own already with them. Michelle, Jessica and Heather were all sitting together between the two men, deeper inside the alcove. When I arrived with the drinks, everyone shifted to make room for me.

I was briefly flummoxed to find myself squeezing in next to Roarr rather than Loke, but the activity of squeezing in together had missed Loke's attention entirely. Mainly because he seemed fascinated with the room around us.

I was pretty sure he was examining our magical handiwork. But from the neutral expression on his face, I had no idea what he was thinking about what he saw.

"So, what do you think?" Jessica asked as Heather delicately wiped a bit of mead from her lips.

"It's very sweet," she said after a moment's thought.

"But not too sweet," Jessica said.

"No, not too sweet," Heather agreed. But I didn't think she meant it. She was thirstily eyeing the mug of ale in front of Roarr. Not that he noticed.

"So you've hired Heather to help in the café," I said to Jessica. "I take it that means business has been good?"

"Business has been very good," Jessica said. "But there is a bare patch on my art wall." She pulled an innocent face, then took a long sip from her glass of mead.

"I swear I'm going to get on that," I said.

"Ingrid has so much on her plate, Jess," Michelle said admonishingly.

"True, but I actually do have some pieces for you," I admitted. "I just haven't gotten around to getting them to Andrew so he can frame them."

"Oh, no hurry," Jessica said. For some reason, she was blushing furiously, but trying to cover it up by taking another hurried sip of mead. Then Heather did the same, although she couldn't quite keep her distaste from her face as she sat back.

"Roarr, trade spots with me," I said, poking him in the side. He had fallen into the sort of starting into the glass reverie more common with lonely drunks sitting by themselves at the end of a bar. But he snapped back into the moment at my poke and got up to let me slide past him to sit closer to Michelle.

"Hey, you," she said. "Excited for the wedding?"

"You know about the wedding?" I asked.

"Word gets around," she said airily. Then leaned closer to my ear to say, "Of course your grandmother told me. I only know Kara a little, and I've never met Thorge at all, but they're close friends of yours, right?"

"Some of the closest," I said. "Present company accepted."

"Of course," she said, and touched her mead glass to mine.

But something going on at the other end of the table caught my eye as I sipped at my mead. Not from Loke, who still seemed to be as studiously staring off into space as Roarr was contemplating the bottom of his full mug of ale. No, something had changed the mood between Jessica and Heather. They were whispering together, and Jessica was rubbing at Heather's back as if lending comfort.

But for her part, Heather was looking a little freaked out. She was also slouching lower in her chair, although being in the deepest part of the alcove, she could scarcely be seen by the rest of the crowd inside the mead hall.

"What's going on?" I asked. But I didn't say this out loud. I only whispered it to Michelle.

And, Michelle being Michelle, she knew I was talking about more than the sudden change in mood.

She leaned closer to me, making sure the back of her head was to Jessica and Heather huddled together, and rolled her eyes. Then she whispered close to my ear, "Heather isn't so much an employee as a project."

"A project?" I whispered back.

"Do you call it a damsel in distress if the rescuer is another damsel?" she pondered.

"Sure," I said. Why not?

"I don't know all the details, but Jessica created this position just for Heather, to help her out. She wasn't exactly hiring, although I'm sure she could use the help. No, she just has this sudden driving need to build good karma or something."

"Why?" I asked. I couldn't think of a single thing I could even imagine Jessica doing that would be described as drawing *bad* karma. So why the need to counter it?

Michelle just shrugged. "Personally, I was hoping it was just because she's been a little lonely."

"Why is she lonely?" I asked.

Michelle gave me a nervously chagrined smile. "That's my bad. I mean, she's been busy in the café, sure enough. But I've been taking online courses. I'm hoping to get a business degree before I take over the restaurant from my mother. Whenever that happens." She gave a careless shrug, but my enthusiastic embrace ruined her attempts at looking nonchalant.

"That's fantastic, Michelle!" I said, squeezing her tight.

"It is," she agreed. "But it's also a lot more work than I planned for. And it will be, for months to come, I'm sure. Anyway, enter Heather, I guess," she said with another shrug.

"You're not jealous, are you?" I asked, in so low of a whisper I had to say it twice before Michelle caught it.

"No, not at all," she said. She went to take a sip of mead, found the glass empty, and pushed it back across the table. "I just think they got awfully close awfully fast is all. But, you know what? Not my business."

I wished I had her attitude. Because to me, it felt like totally my business. I wasn't going to let some newcomer warp my friend.

Even if it was a friend I hadn't exactly been there for in months. If ever.

"It's okay, he's gone now," Jessica said, her voice carrying more loudly than she intended in a momentary lapse in the noise around us.

"Who's gone now?" I asked, looking around the hall.

"No one," Heather said, too quickly.

"What's up?" Roarr asked, instantly out of his stupor. Loke was focusing on the rest of us again too, although he said nothing.

"There's a guy who's been hanging around the café trying to see Heather," Jessica said, her jaw as tense as I had ever seen it.

"A guy?" Roarr asked, leaning forward ever so slightly.

"Don't worry. I handled it," Jessica said. "He's not a bad guy, really. He just needed someone to remind him of... I don't know. He just needed to get things back into perspective. Which he has. Look, he's heading out the door now. He knows he overstepped by coming here."

I looked towards the Runde door, but it was already swinging closed again. I hadn't caught even a glimpse of who we were talking about.

"What's his name?" I asked. Perhaps a bit too forcefully.

Why was I feeling so on-edge? It was like the whole evening, instead of enjoying time with my friends, I was hunting for problems to be solved, mysteries to investigate, or fights to throw myself into.

I glanced up at the spellwork above us and told myself I was being silly.

But Loke was looking up too, as if following my gaze. What did he see that I didn't?

"You know what? It's totally a problem I've dealt with, so we can let it drop," Jessica said, looking over at Heather. Heather gave her a timid nod, then a second, more confident one.

"Jess—" I started to say.

"Ingrid, if you want to stop by the café tomorrow, I can tell you everything. Set your mind at ease. I wanted to talk to you anyway, about other stuff," she said, ending in a mumble. Not looking at me. She was fidgeting with a mead glass that was as empty as Michelle's.

But then she met my eyes with her usual warm, completely genuine smile, and said, "But not tonight. Tonight is for hanging out with no worries except who's going to fetch us some refills. Right, Michelle?"

"Absolutely!" Michelle agreed. "I just turned in my last assignments for the semester, and I have a couple of weeks before the next one rolls in to crush me. In the meantime, it's time for a little kicking back with my friends."

Jessica reached past Heather to give Michelle a quick hug while Loke lunged to grab the empty glasses before they could be elbowed over. Then he whisked them away, disappearing from the table in the blink of an eye in a way that wasn't quite magical.

He was back soon with second rounds for everybody, although Roarr and I were both still on our firsts. I didn't mind. I didn't need the warm glow of mead in my veins to feel completely content in that moment.

I had missed my grandmother's mead hall so much.

That hall was now elbow-to-elbow with people from Runde and Villmark both. So many people had come in through those two sets of doors in the few moments I hadn't been looking.

Now the hall was filled with the sounds of scores of people all talking and laughing together. With the smells of mead and ale that were already starting to slosh and dry stickily on the tables, benches and flagstone floors. With the warmth of so many bodies in what had moments before felt like such a large space.

It almost felt perfect. Almost. I was just asking myself what still felt missing—it couldn't be Thorbjorn, because he had so seldom ever come down to my grandmother's mead hall I didn't associate it with him, and missing him was an entirely different category of feeling—when I felt a hand on my shoulder.

And turned to look up at Andrew.

CHAPTER SIX

I HADN'T EXACTLY FORGOTTEN about Andrew. Or at least that's what I told myself. But I knew the minute my eyes met his that he had been the missing thing that I hadn't been able to put a finger on.

And, yeah, not being able to put a finger on it? That's an awful lot like forgetting.

"Hi, Ingrid," he said almost shyly, and I got up from my chair to give him a hug.

He must've come straight from his woodworking studio. I could smell the fresh smell of wood chips and sawdust with just the faintest undertone of the beeswax he used to season that wood. He wasn't wearing his usual fisherman's sweater, just a clean and new-feeling blue T-shirt, but it *was* nearly Midsummer.

I stepped back from the hug to smile up at him. The thick locks of his dark blond hair were neatly combed, but my fingers didn't feel their usual itch to touch it.

The whole vibe between us felt different. But perhaps that was to be expected, after so many months apart.

"It's good to see you," I said.

There was no reason why those bland words should trigger any sort of memory, and yet they did. I had a sudden full-sensory flash-back to what hadn't even been the last moment I'd seen him, just perhaps the most significant.

It was of the night before I had left Runde for Villmark to start my magical studies under Haraldr rather than just with my grandmother. It was of the very moment we had said goodbye, not sure when or if we'd ever see each other again.

It was of the moment when we had so nearly shared a kiss.

A shiver ran up my spine, but only because the night I was flashing back to had been so chilly. The memory of the near-kiss brought with it no sense of longing or regret. All I felt was a soft sort of nostalgia. As if I were my grandmother's age, looking back at a boy I'd liked back in my schooldays.

I don't know how much of that was written on my face, but the quizzical look Andrew gave me told me clearly the amount had not been zero.

"It's been too long," I said as I fumbled back into my chair and reached for my barely touched mug of mead.

Andrew looked down at me for a long, frozen moment. Was he thinking of the same moment I was? Did it feel different for him?

Was this going to get weird?

But then he just gave my shoulder another squeeze, then pulled a chair from a nearby table to wedge himself between Jessica and Loke.

Loke, who was clearly laughing at me with his dark, dancing eyes. That non-zero amount of what I was thinking that had shown on my face just then? Loke had definitely understood a lot more of it than Andrew had.

He always did.

Then Nilda and Kara were joining us, squeezing in around Roarr, although he still didn't say much. He didn't even drink much. He just sat among us, quietly absorbing the camaraderie around him.

But I didn't mind. Somehow, it just felt like he belonged there. And I supposed whether I spent the rest of my days in Villmark or in Runde or moving between the two, he would always be there. In the background, maybe, but there all the same.

The sound level around us picked up several notches as the

singing and dancing started. I had never seen anyone arrive at the mead hall with an instrument on them, and when I roamed the room before or after everyone was there, I had never seen a stash of them anywhere about the place. And yet every night music would just... happen. Sometimes it was a honkytonk piano, sometimes it was old Viking songs not entirely unlike sea chanties, and sometimes it was a rock band or even karaoke. I guess the person who started it determined the genre, but I had never once seen it happen.

I wasn't even sure which of the network of spells my grandmother and I wove over the hall triggered this phenomenon. I made a mental note to check the next time we touched the magic.

That night, it was a jukebox suddenly appearing near the main fireplace at the far end of the room. And that jukebox was loaded with dance hits from the 90s.

I was really curious who triggered that.

The driving beat of a song I knew well—and yet couldn't name the title or artist to save my life—filled the hall, and Michelle and Jessica both gave shrieks of joy. Michelle was up on her feet like her chair had been suddenly electrified, and she grabbed Jessica by both hands to drag her to the open space closer to the middle of the hall.

The music was too loud for me to hear what Jessica said over her shoulder to Andrew. Probably an invitation to join them. But he just shook his head and waved his hands both, emphatically refusing to join them. He briefly caught my eye but dropped his gaze down into his ale mug as if my eyes had burned him somehow.

And Loke was still smirking.

Heather lingered for a moment, looking over again and again at Andrew as if hoping to catch his attention. But when that failed to happen, she got up to join Michelle and Jessica on the impromptu dance floor by the fireplace.

"It's good to be back. Isn't it?" Roarr leaned close to my ear to say. Nilda and Kara had also gotten up to dance, leaving open spaces he had slid across to sit beside me.

"It is," I agreed. But he was giving me a look I couldn't quite read. I raised a questioning eyebrow, and he leaned over again to speak close to my ear.

"You look like it's all a bit much," he said. Even speaking close to my ear, he had to shout to be heard over the beat of the music.

That was the loudest jukebox I had ever encountered, that was for sure.

But Roarr's steady gaze was waiting for my answer. So I leaned close to his ear to say, "It's just loud."

"Not like Villmark," he said in my ear.

"No, not like Villmark," I agreed. Then I sat back in my chair and reached for my mead. Which I didn't exactly want. As good as it was, I was too tired and too unused to staying up late at all. Just the contents of one glass of my grandmother's mead would have me putting my head down on that table and going right to sleep, never mind the music.

The noise level wasn't the only thing that was different in Villmark. My sleep schedule had shifted so gradually I hadn't even noticed it until that minute. But after months of meditations at sunrise—and no need to stay awake deep into the night working on art projects that always came behind too many shifts at the diner like I had done routinely before moving to Runde after art school—I had become the kind of person who went to bed at a reasonable hour.

But my grandmother? For as long as I'd known her, she'd been a night owl. Even when it had just been the two of us on the lake shore in that isolated cabin with no people anywhere around us, no TV or internet or even radio to distract us, my grandmother had always been awake until deep into the night.

Normally, none of this would be any kind of problem. Especially now that we didn't even live together.

But I had promised to be there to help close the hall up for the night. To help batten down the spells to the slumbering status in which they would pass through the day until the next sundown.

And it was barely ten o'clock. I was never going to make it.

I realized that Andrew was trying to catch my attention and

looked up at him. I couldn't hear a word he said, but he enunciated it slowly, pointing with both thumbs towards the Runde door.

"Do you want to get some fresh air?"

I'm pretty sure that's what I was lip-reading, anyway. I gave a grateful nod and followed him away from the table, then past the dance floor where everyone was whooping in hearty appreciation of whatever song's opening was being mixed in with the last song's final bars.

Heather was doing some serious old school dance moves, more 90s nostalgia-triggering than even the music. And beside her, Jessica was matching her move for move.

I quickly shifted my awareness to the magical realm, just to be sure. But nothing magical was going on between them. Jessica wasn't under any kind of spell.

But she wasn't exactly acting like herself, either.

"Ingrid?" Andrew called back when he realized he was leaving me behind. I turned too quickly in my effort to rush over to him and collided with a solid wall of chest. I bounced off it and nearly stumbled backwards, but a firm grip on my arm kept me on my feet.

"Sorry!" I said, looking up at the man I had run into. He was no one I recognized, and I would've remembered that thick, curly brown hair and even darker brown eyes if I had met him before. But he was clearly a Runde resident, dressed in jeans, a button-up shirt and boots. Not that he looked like he'd just come in off the lake or from a long day of farm labor. His shirt was crisply pressed, and his boots were polished to a high shine.

"No worries," he said, letting me go when he could see I was steady on my own feet.

"Ingrid," Andrew said again, having come back to retrieve me.

"Sorry!" I said to the young man again as Andrew drew me away.

I wanted to talk to Andrew, and getting away from the relentless beat of the music would do my head good.

But I was a little worried I was rushing when I should be staying to examine that man a little more carefully. I was positive that when I had collided with him, he hadn't seen me coming because he'd been watching Michelle, Jessica and Heather on the dance floor.

I mean, I couldn't be a hundred percent sure, and I was feeling extra paranoid that evening, especially with anything dealing with Jessica.

For no reason. But I shelved that mental concern to ponder later.

Also, a single guy in a drinking establishment watching attractive women dancing together wasn't exactly the weirdest thing in the world. And I had gotten no creepy vibes from him. Not even when I'd plastered myself up against him.

And the mead hall's protective magic was in perfect working order. I had nothing to be worried about.

Except, maybe, for the conversation I was about to have. And, honestly, avoiding thinking about that was probably why I was so fixated on dealing with anyone else's problems at all, real or imaginary.

But the time had come.

Andrew and I finally burst out of the meeting hall doors into the parking lot full of pickups and SUVs. The air was debatably fresher, but definitely cooler. I hadn't realized how flushed I was from the heat until the breeze brought sweet relief to my hot cheeks.

The heavy doors banged shut behind us, and the music was dampened down to a mere hint of a beat in a shapeless warble of bass. I could hear the sound of someone's steps, someone not quite in view of the flickering parking lot light. They were either walking to their car or just catching a breath of fresh air away from the music like the two of us were doing.

Without a word, the two of us started walking down the dirt road that lead from the mead hall, past the beginnings of my grandmother's cabin, and towards the shore of Lake Superior beyond.

"You look well," Andrew said, a little more loudly than I'm sure he expected. But then his ears were probably ringing just like mine were.

"Well?" I repeated lamely. His words weren't as confusing as his body language, though. He was walking beside me, but he was being careful to leave a sizable gap between us. And his hands were jammed firmly down into his pockets. What was he afraid was going to happen?

"I mean good, of course," he said, closer to a normal volume now.

"So do you," I said. But that was as much small talk as I could muster. I found myself blathering out, "Is it weird, me being back here? It's weird, isn't it? It feels weird."

"It's a little weird," he said with the hint of a smile to the corner of his mouth.

"It's been too long," I said with a sigh. "I haven't even been to the café yet. And there's no way I'm staying the night in that," I added, pointing to my grandmother's mobile home as we strolled past it. "I'll have to go back to Villmark after I help close up."

"But you'll be back tomorrow?" he asked. I couldn't quite read his tone. It wasn't eager, or an earnest wish to know when he'd see me again, I was pretty sure. But in the darkness of the mostly unlit road, the half moon not yet risen over the lake, his face was only a glow of sweat from the too-warm mead hall still drying as we walked.

"I don't know," I admitted. "I hope so. But it will be one day at a time."

"Sure," he said, nodding a little too emphatically in agreement. We scrunched over the gravel that was deeper where we were on the edge of the road. Then he said, "So you've been hanging out with Roarr?"

"Hanging out?" I repeated. "With Roarr? Why would you think that?"

"He was there, inside," he said, gesturing back at the brightest source of light behind us. "You two were talking."

"Not *talking* talking," I said. Then I couldn't help but laughing. Which only made the awkwardness between us worse. I put a hand over my own mouth until I had it under control. "Roarr was just there. That's all."

"Okay," Andrew said. But for some reason, that declaration of mine seemed to be disappointing him somehow.

"I haven't forgotten what he's done," I said. Andrew, Michelle and Jessica had all been friends with Lisa, Roarr's now-dead fiancée.

"No! Of course not!" he said, and stopped walking so suddenly I had to turn to take a few steps back to stand before him. "I wasn't thinking about that at all."

"So, what were you thinking?" I asked.

He was looking at my feet, like he deliberately wouldn't look up at my eyes. Then he gave me a very lame shrug. "I don't know. It's been a long time. I thought you'd…. I don't know what I thought."

Which wasn't true. We *both* knew what he'd thought. He thought Roarr and I were a couple now.

And I was on the verge of inappropriate laughing all over again. "Sorry," I said, when he risked looking up at me long enough to shoot me an alarmed look. I stopped the chuckles before they really got going. "Sorry, it's just… you thought Roarr before you thought Loke?"

"You and Loke are—" he started to say. He was looking up at me again. It was hard to tell in the darkness, but I'd swear it was relief washing over his face in that moment.

"Just friends. Same as always," I said. "I can't really say the same about Roarr, though. A little less than friends. I don't know what vibes you were picking up."

"Nothing. No vibes," he said. Now he was sounding all defensive, for no reason I could tell.

"Andrew, what are we talking about right now?" I asked in desperation.

Before he could formulate an answer, the doors to the hall banged open and I could hear Jessica calling our names. Louder than she needed to, even with the music spilling out around her as she stood holding both doors open and scanning the darkness for the two of us.

Then Heather appeared at her side, also calling out, but only shouting Andrew's name.

"Over here!" Andrew called back. Then he walked away from me without answering my question.

I didn't follow. I just stood there, massaging my temples against a building headache. I didn't want to go back inside, at all. Although I wasn't sure which was worse: the loud music or the palpable awkwardness.

Never mind, actually. I knew which. It was definitely the latter.

Andrew had thought Roarr and I were a couple? In what universe was that even a reasonable possibility?

The door opened again, spilling dance music out into the night. At first, I thought Jessica was coming out to get me. I quickly amended that to Heather coming outside for whatever reason. But it was neither of them. Just some other young woman about the same size with about the same hairstyle.

Well, it was a popular look. It was possible Heather and Jessica looking so much alike was just a coincidence. And I was jumping at shadows.

Those words had no sooner formed in my mind than I literally was jumping at shadows. Or at least a voice that suddenly emerged from the shadows.

"You can't hide out here forever, you know."

Then Loke was standing in front of me. Because of course he was. And he was probably still smirking at me too, although I didn't drop my hands to look up at him to see.

"I don't suppose if I asked you what was going on that you'd give me a straight answer?" I said.

"Not on your life," he said. I still wasn't looking at him. But that thing in cartoons where the wolf's grin unfurls ever wider and you can hear it?

Apparently, that's a real thing. Because I could hear Loke, grinning at me like a wolf.

"But you know," I said. Not even a question.

He just shrugged. "You and I both know that I never know as much as I pretend to."

"That's true," I agreed.

"But I'm a terribly accurate guesser. I can conjecture with the best of them," he said as he slipped his arm through mine to walk me back to the mead hall doors. "But don't ask me to do it now. You and I are looking at the same clues, after all. I don't know a thing that you haven't had the same opportunity to observe as I have. You just need to look a little closer."

"Okay, just tell me one thing," I said. He said nothing, so I pressed on. "Who in the nine worlds would ever believe I was together with Roarr?"

Loke laughed a little too heartily at that. "That's a very good question. A very good question. You should ponder that."

Then he opened the doors and pulled me back inside the mead hall.

Where he knew full well the driving beats of 90's dance songs were too overwhelming for me to question him further.

CHAPTER SEVEN

MY EARS WERE STILL RINGING LONG after the last of the customers had left at two in the morning. I knew it was from the music, even though the jukebox had faded away not long after midnight. But it kind of felt like my driving exhaustion had become an audible tone.

"Do you want me to stay?" Kara asked as Nilda waited for her near the Villmark door.

"No, dear, we should have it just fine without you," my grandmother said to her. Then she kissed her on the cheek and smiled at her. "You did very well this evening, but I think the rest of your training will wait until after your wedding."

"My mind was disordered, wasn't it?" Kara fretted. "I knew I wasn't focusing."

"I wouldn't have said you did very well if you hadn't," my grandmother said sternly. But then she softened again. "Not like anyone could blame you for your mind being a little unfocused at the moment. It was good for you to be here for the anchoring of the spells, but for the next few days, you should focus just on your wedding. We'll pick up your training after you and Thorge have settled into your new lives together."

"You're sure?" Kara asked. But Nilda had already opened the door and the sounds of the frogs from the river just out of sight to the south of the hall filled the air.

"I'm sure," my grandmother said. "Have a good night. And I'll see you on your wedding day."

"Two days away now," Kara said with a happy smile. Then she hugged each of us before running to join her sister.

Loke was there with them now too, raising a hand in a silent farewell. I was tempted to pull him back and make him wait for me, but I didn't think he'd submit to that quietly.

But I could always find him tomorrow. One way or the other, he was going to tell me what his guesses and conjectures about Andrew were.

The frog sound cut off abruptly as the door swung shut, then my grandmother and I were left alone in the mead hall.

"Clean up?" I asked, trying—and failing—not to sound as tired as I felt.

"You weren't paying attention to the spells we were weaving at all?" she asked me. I couldn't tell if her tone was legitimately stern or if she were just pretending to be stern in jest.

In such cases, it was best to just answer honestly and see how she reacted.

"I recognized the ones I paid the most attention to before," I said slowly. "The ones that hide the hall and muffle it in the memories of the Runde residents. I could see the tweaks you made with the old ones."

"But you didn't see the new ones at all?" she asked, her tone still in that nebulous zone.

"No?" I admitted, not quite flinching.

"We'll have to go over them all the next time we bring them up, when I'm less distracted by the work itself," she said. She wasn't angry with me; I could finally relax.

And notice that half of the hall around me had mysteriously become clean while I was focused on her. I turned in a slow circle, and by the time I was facing her again, more of the cleaning had been done. The mugs and glasses were in gleaming rows behind the bar, the tables still had streaks from where rags had recently wiped them clean, and the floor was freshly mopped as well.

"Handy," I said.

"I thought so," my grandmother said drily. "It should just take a moment and then we can shut things down for the night. Then I get to sleep in; the Sorensen boys can handle the opening of the general store and post office in the morning without me."

"You've really thought this through," I said. "I'm glad you're being sure to take care of yourself."

She made a noncommittal sound, then said, "You'll keep that in mind, I trust, when the council grills you tomorrow."

"I'm supposed to report on you to the council tomorrow?" I asked. That was news to me.

"I'm certain they'll each drop by casually with their questions," she said, and I was sure she was right.

I turned in another slow circle but could see no sign of cleaning still in progress or still to be done. "I think we're ready," I said.

"I agree," she said, and moved to join me in the center of the room. I had already shifted my vision from its normal range into one where I could better perceive the spells all around me. They were like luminous threads surrounding me, woven like fabric up the walls, then netted like dense layers of spiderwebs overhead.

"Ready?" my grandmother asked me. She had already raised her arms to start the work.

"Ready," I said, raising my own arms.

I knew at once that something had gone wrong. The energy that should've been flowing into me freely just wasn't there. At first I chalked this up to my own tiredness. My ears were still ringing from the overly loud music, and that was making it hard to focus.

I took a slow breath in and out, then tried again. But this time, the lack of flow was more pronounced. Like I could almost sense some sort of magical dam holding that energy back from me.

I heard my grandmother make a grunt of effort and realized she couldn't touch anything either.

Conversation inside of spellwork is possible, but it's always distracting. And with the level of spells we were working with now, any distraction could be a really bad thing. So I said nothing, just shifted my awareness to more closely perceive what my grandmother was doing.

But what she was doing was struggling. At first, it was like the struggle of a parent trying to bring a mid-tantrum toddler back under control, but even as I watched, it morphed. Now it was like she was grappling with an opponent in some sort of magical Greco-Roman wrestling match.

So I broke the rule and spoke out loud. "Perhaps we should just leave it," I said. "It might be easier to do in the morning."

As much as I knew my grandmother needed that sleep-in she was planning for the morning, and as much as I didn't want to be up at dawn myself, it felt like the wisest course.

But she continued fighting with the spells, pulling down the threads by great fistfuls. She didn't answer me at first, just kept pulling and pulling. But the threads wouldn't unbind from each other, and they wouldn't break.

She was starting to look alarmingly like an insect about to be irrevocably bound inside that spiderweb.

"Mormor, stop!" I pleaded.

But she still didn't answer. All my hair stood on end as I felt her draw in more power than I had ever taken in at one moment. She directed all of it towards the nexus of the spells at the highest point of the mead hall roof above us.

The light was blinding, and the blast wave that followed it knocked me down to the—thankfully clean—flagstone floor. I blinked again and again before my vision finally cleared enough for me to see.

My grandmother was still standing, but her face had gone ashen gray, and her hands were on her knees as she fought for breath.

And beyond her, the spells glowed as pristine and bright as ever before. Not a thread had failed to move back into place. It was like my grandmother had done nothing at all.

And yet I could see just from looking at her she had done far more than she should've done.

"Mormor?" I called, still sitting on the floor. I wasn't feeling steady enough to get up just yet.

She raised her head enough to look at me. The panic I felt building inside me quieted a little at the fierce determination in her eyes. She wasn't afraid or worried. She was just ready to move this skirmish up to a proper battle.

She pushed off her knees to straighten up and was just about to speak when the door to Villmark banged open so loudly we both jumped.

"Something's happened!" Loke gasped, nearly out of breath.

"We've got it under control," my grandmother said.

But my instincts screamed at me that Loke wasn't talking about the mead hall at all. Then he confirmed it by looking around in mild surprise that the illusions that made the place look like a Viking-era hall still held.

"What is it?" I asked him.

"The cave," he said, pointing back over his own shoulder.

"The cave to Villmark?" I asked, and finally pushed up off the ground to stand.

But my grandmother was already moving. Her walking stick appeared out of nowhere before she was halfway to the door. She took a firm grip on Loke's elbow and propelled him before her across the patio and up the path that led to the waterfall.

I jogged to get close enough to be heard and asked the both of them, "Is this because of the mead hall spells? Mormor, did you pull from Loke?"

Because draining too much of his latent magic power could've crippled his portal traveling thing. I guessed.

"It's not me!" Loke insisted.

"Tell me what happened," my grandmother said even as we reached the point in the path where it grew so steep hands were needed as much as feet.

"You saw us leave, and we came straight here," Loke said as he climbed. "I didn't sense anything wrong. Nothing at all. Kara and Nilda were walking a little ahead of me through the cavern, and I saw them make the turn past the cave unblocked by the stone to the cavern with the ancestral fire in it. I could see their shadows on the wall, I swear it. But when I got there, there was nothing."

"They were gone?" I asked, nearly winded from the climb. But we had reached the cavern behind the waterfall. We had had a rather wet spring, and the water levels were still up. The roar of falling water was louder than I had ever heard it. And yet it was a comfort. It was so loud it drowned out the ringing that lingered in my ears, and was a much more soothing sound.

But it wasn't exactly easy to hear over, and whatever Loke was saying was lost to me. I caught his elbow and pulled him to face me.

"They were gone?" I repeated.

"Yes, but not just Kara and Nilda," he said. "The cave is gone. The fire is gone. All of it."

"What?" I demanded.

But my grandmother was already inside the cave at the far side of the cavern. We ran to catch up with her as she stood with her walking stick firmly planted between her feet and both her hands gripping it tightly. She was staring at the stone before her with a dark glower.

"The cave is gone," Loke said again, and his words finally sank in. The cave took a turn here, away from Runde and towards Villmark. It was meant to lead into the cavern where the ancestral fire was kept always burning. In times when more defense was needed, the Thors who guarded the fire would roll the stone across the cave mouth just where we were standing to block the entrance to Villmark.

But that stone wasn't what we were looking at. No, what we were looking at was the unmarred wall of a cave that went nowhere. There was no mouth to a deeper cave for the stone to block.

"You saw this change occur?" my grandmother asked Loke sharply as she ran one palm over the surface of the rock. I did the same. It felt like rock, just normal rock. I could see no signs of spells. It was just like the village of Villmark had never existed at all, or at least this entrance to it never had.

"I saw the dancing light of the fire on the wall here," he said, pointing to the opposite side of the cave. "I saw Kara and Nilda's shadows there, sharp at first and then blurrier as they grew smaller. Then I guess I blinked or something, but in the next instant it was all gone. There was nothing left but this."

"What does this mean?" I asked my grandmother. She studied the stone walls a bit longer, then just shook her head.

"It's not even the worst part," Loke said.

"What's the worst part?" I asked.

But it was my grandmother who answered. "He can't get home by his own methods either," she said.

I looked at Loke, and the anguish in his eyes was so palpable I knew that my grandmother was right.

"I tried and tried, before I opened the door properly into the mead hall," he said in a harsh whisper. "But I couldn't make it do it. I couldn't make it take me home. I couldn't make it take me to anywhere in Villmark. I'm stuck here."

I pulled him into a tight hug. I felt him stiffen in resistance at first, then let me hug him. Then finally he hugged me back, letting me hold him up if just for a moment.

I knew he was thinking about Esja. His sister who was sick more often than she was well.

His sister who was now completely alone.

"We're going to get you back," I promised him. "We're going to get you back to your sister."

I made that vow with all my heart and soul.

I just didn't know how I was going to pull it off.

CHAPTER EIGHT

AT MY GRANDMOTHER'S BEHEST, I walked Loke back down to Runde, past the darkened mead hall to my grandmother's trailer in the parking lot. She remained behind in the cave to study the problem further on her own.

As much as I might have wanted to stay and help her, to see if I could solve the problem using my own magic if she had no luck with hers, I didn't have the heart to even say so out loud.

I had never seen Loke so distraught. The raw emotions radiating off him were a chaotic mess. Panic and shock were still drowning out most of the others, but I could feel the anger inside him growing.

My grandmother was right. He needed to be distracted. At least until she was finished investigating things. His presence was too over-whelming for her to concentrate properly. The magic he had so little control over was still a powerful force. And I could feel him disrupting it again and again as he fought to open a doorway back to his home.

He let me guide him into the trailer, but then he immediately started pacing. Back and forth, back and forth across the far too tiny space.

I went into the kitchen, where I was mostly out of his way. "Can I get you anything?" I offered and started opening cupboards and the refrigerator to take an inventory.

"Coffee," he said, almost a snap as he stalked past me in his very aggressive form of pacing the central hall.

"Coffee," I repeated.

I could totally do coffee. The maker was right there on the tiny counter, the ground beans in the canister beside it. I just wasn't sure that putting caffeine in him wasn't going to turn out to be a very bad idea.

"Coffee," he said again as he went past me the other way. "I won't rest until I know Esja is all right."

"How was she when you saw her last?" I asked. "I mean, you never would've come down to the mead hall if she was having one of her bad days."

"No, she was fine. But that can change in a flash," he said, and snapped his fingers loudly to punctuate his point.

"Sure," I agreed. I had put a fresh liner in the coffeemaker and was holding a scoop of ground beans over it, but I couldn't quite get my hand to commit.

But in the end I made a full pot of double-strength coffee. Partly because I had a vague hope that it was like giving coffee to some people I had known with ADHD back in art school, where it really seemed to even them out.

But mostly because it was past two in the morning, and I didn't know when I'd be seeing my own bed again, and I really, really needed it.

As I stood there, tapping my fingers on my crossed arms as I watched the machine brew, I heard the doors in the back of the trailer open and close a few times. Then there was silence, just long enough to start a glimmer of worry in my mind.

Then Loke was back again, pacing back me towards the front of the trailer.

"Nothing?" I asked.

"I can hop around Runde and the rest of the modern world, but Villmark and everything beyond it is closed off to me," he said.

"We're going to figure this out," I said, even as my grandmother opened the trailer door and climbed up the steps inside. She leaned her walking stick in the corner, then looked at the two of us standing there as if she had no idea why we were inside her mobile home.

"Coffee?" I offered.

"No," she said in an automatic sort of way. Then she seemed to really hear me and changed her answer to, "Yes, actually. I have a feeling I'm going to need it."

I added a third mug to the other two waiting on the counter, then watched the last few drops of coffee drip down before pulling out the carafe to pour.

It wasn't quite the consistency of sludge, but it was definitely far blacker than my usual French roast. All three of us gathered around the table in the kitchen and downed large gulps of the coffee we were all taking black. I shivered at the bitterness, but the caffeine hit me almost at once.

It might be a fake kind of wakefulness, but it was a welcome one.

"What now?" Loke asked after taking a second gulp from his mug.

"Now, I would say the two of you might as well get some rest, but after this brew, I don't think that's likely," my grandmother said.

"What are you going to do?" I asked her.

"I need to work on some things on my own, dear," she said, putting her hand on mine and giving it a little squeeze.

"So you want us to go?" I asked, not sure where we would even go. There were no hotels in Runde. And everyone I knew still more or less lived with their parents.

"No, you two can stay here. I'm going back inside the mead hall," she said.

"Is that really the problem you want to solve first?" Loke asked almost venomously. I started to admonish him, but my grandmother's hand on mine gave a second squeeze, this one asking for my silence.

"The two are related, I'm afraid," she said. "And it's really on me to solve them both. Ingrid doesn't know the spells the way I do."

"But there must be something we can do to help," I said. "I helped put it up, after all. Shouldn't I be a part of taking it all down again?"

"Until I know what must be done, I don't know what you can do to help," she said tiredly. Then she drained the last of her coffee and got up to rinse out the mug in the little sink.

"What about me?" Loke asked. "What if I let you pull everything out of me? Drain me to a husk, I don't care. Just fix this."

"Loke, surely it won't come to that," I said to him.

"I hope it won't," my grandmother said. "But I appreciate the offer."

"Mormor!" I gasped.

"I hope it won't come to that," she said again, hands raised in surrender. "But honestly, there is no point in continuing this conversation until I've investigated further. And this is my mead hall. The spells are mine. The building is mine. No one can fix this if I cannot."

"How long do you think that's going to take?" Loke asked.

"I don't know, but I'll be done sooner if I start sooner," she said. She dried her hands on the kitchen towel, then gave us both a sad, tired look. "I still think the best thing the two of you can do is rest up. It's very likely I'll need both of you at full energy, and staying up all night fretting isn't going to get you there. But it doesn't matter what I say, you'll make your own choices. So I'll just say good night for now."

"Wake us when you need us," I said as she headed for the door. She stopped to give me a curt nod, and then she was gone.

"The spells were different," Loke said the minute the door had banged shut behind her. "I was looking at them all night. Half of them, I couldn't even guess at what they were meant to do."

"None of them were bad," I said. "I felt all the magic flowing through me. If she had been putting in curses or whatever, I would've sensed that. It was just spells to make running the mead hall easier. That's all."

"That's what you think is true, anyway. No offense, Ingrid, but you're still really new at all this," he said.

"Believe me, that's a fact that's never far from the front of my mind," I said, then got up to refill my coffee cup. Loke pushed his own empty mug towards me without a word, and I filled it for him. But then we both just sat at the little table, hands wrapped around the warm ceramic mugs, staring down into the tar-like contents without speaking.

"Maybe you could try drawing something," he said after several long minutes of silence.

"Like what?" I asked. "The mead hall? The cavern? All of Runde and Villmark?"

"Any of it? All of it?" he said. Then he gave a frustrated shrug.

I went to find my bag where I had left it on one of the ugly chairs in the living area, then came back with a sketchbook and pencils. I sketched the outlines of the mead hall from memory, then the same location in its Runde guise as a meeting hall. I drew the river and the waterfall and the cavern behind the waterfall.

They were decent sketches, but the magical flow was beyond elusive. Nothing was pulling me in or speaking to me at all.

Loke said nothing, just sipped his coffee as he watched me draw, then turn a page and draw again.

"Maybe you need to go look at it again," he suggested when I set my pencil down to get yet a third cup of middle-of-the-night coffee.

"Maybe," I said, but not like I believed it. "Maybe all this caffeine is inhibiting my abilities. I don't know."

"I left with Nilda and Kara just before you and Nora started trying to pull down the spells," Loke mused.

"We didn't start straight away," I said, sitting back down with my coffee. I picked up my pencil but just sort of fidgeted with it, making random lines on the paper.

"No, I'm guessing you started just about the time the three of us reached the cavern," Loke said. "The two of them got through, but then something you did changed something. The timing is so exact, it can't be coincidental, right?"

"It's not like we synchronized our watches or anything," I said, looking at him more than at the page before me, although my hand kept practicing lines. "We have no way of knowing just how exact that timing was. And anyway, if it was because of the spells, why didn't everything lock down when we cast them in the first place? Why did it only lock down when we tried to pull them down for the night?"

"Some self-protective instinct of the magic itself?" Loke said. "Maybe you accidentally summoned something that didn't want to go away again so soon."

"Well, it's not like we kill anything when we pull the spells down for the night," I said. "The spells still exist. They're just sort of sleeping. Like banking embers for the night in a hearth. You don't have to light a fire again in the morning. You just have to stir it back to life."

"Everyone got home but me," Loke said darkly. "That's the only other thing I can think. That somehow this is about me."

"Well, I don't think that's true," I said.

"You don't know," he countered.

"Neither do you," I said. "You just like thinking the worst. Why don't you go back to blaming me and Mormor?"

"I'm not *blaming* anyone," he said sullenly. Then his eyes fell on the sketchbook on the table in front of me. I looked down to see a scribbly sort of drawing had emerged from my idle pencil marks. I could just discern the outline of Loke's sister Esja, sleeping in a chair by the fireplace in the library of their family home.

"Did you see that or just draw it?" he asked.

"I wasn't thinking about drawing at all. It just came out of me," I said. I pushed the book over to him. "She looks well."

"She looks like she waited up for me, and now she's sleeping in a chair rather than in her own bed," he said.

"She grabbed a wool throw first," I said. "I think she's doing fine."

"For now," he grumbled. But the grumpiness in his tone sounded a little forced. Like he just didn't want to admit that the sketch had made him feel even the tiniest bit better.

I looked down at the mostly untouched third cup of coffee before me. The caffeine I had already had was singing in my veins. But despite that, I was exhausted.

"I think maybe my mormor was right about the need for rest," I admitted.

"You can go lie down. I'll sit up and wait for her to return," he said, pulling my mug towards him and adding its contents to his own mug.

"Are you sure?"

"Yeah. Go ahead," he said, even as he rubbed tiredly at his eyes. "My heart's racing too much for sleep, anyway."

"Mine too, but I'm sure that will slow right down as soon as Mjolner curls up against me and starts purring," I said.

Then an icy fist of fear closed around my heart.

"What is it?" Loke asked, half raising from his chair.

"Mjolner. He's not here," I said.

"That's not unusual, though, right?" Loke said, although I could see my growing panic infecting him too.

I closed my eyes and thought of my polydactyl black cat. I imagined him in every detail, from the green of his eyes to the silver of his namesake hammer that hung from his collar. And I called out to him with every bit of the magic I possessed.

That had never failed to bring him to me in the past. He could walk through walls, he could travel through different planes of existence.

He could always get to my side when I called for him.

But this time, he didn't come. I couldn't even sense him at all. It was like he was gone. It was like he had never been.

And, just as I had done for him in the cavern behind the waterfall, Loke held me tight and lent me all his strength to fight the panic that was so close to consuming me.

The world had suddenly gone very, very wrong.

And I didn't know how we were going to fix it.

CHAPTER NINE

I WOKE UP HORRIBLY DISORIENTED, not the least because I didn't remember falling asleep at all. But at some point Loke and I had moved our vigil from the kitchen to the sofa under the window in the front room. We had sat together going over everything we knew about how magic worked, which was all too little. So we had gone over it again and again.

It was like my memory was caught on an infinite, too-short loop of those same words over and over again.

And then suddenly this: waking with the sun painfully bright in my eyes—having risen high enough to clear the tops of the trees to the east of the trailer windows—and a persistent pounding that it took me far too long to work out was someone knocking on the door. For the longest time, I just thought it was my caffeine-boosted heart rate beating a tattoo inside my very ears.

"Coming," I croaked even as Loke beside me sat up with a start and looked around, as disoriented as I was. I stumbled across the room to the door, which I promptly threw open with too much gusto. It banged loudly against the wall of the trailer. "Sorry," I said, my voice still frog-like, as I blinked out into the morning sun, trying to find the source of the knocking.

It was Andrew. "Ingrid! I thought you'd be... Never mind. I need Nora," he said.

"She's not back," I said, more for my own benefit than his. Yes, that had to be true. She wasn't back yet, or else she would've woken us up. That was why we'd stayed in the living room. So she couldn't slip past us.

"Back from where?" he asked. There was an edge to his voice, and I forced myself to focus on his face. Which was kind of the last thing I wanted to do after the awkwardness of the night before.

But all of that was gone now. With his hair disheveled, his eyes wide and crazy, and his hands twisting together with an intensity that had to be borderline painful, he was exhibiting all the signs of panic that Loke and I had been staving off in ourselves all night long.

But this couldn't have anything to do with the spells, could it? What would Andrew know about it? And why would he care to this extent? No, something else was going on.

Just what I needed. Something else going on.

"What's happened?" I asked, stepping out of the trailer to look around. But he was alone.

"I need Nora," he said.

"Ingrid will have to do," Loke said as he emerged from the trailer behind me to join us on the uneven surface of the parking lot. Andrew almost jumped at his sudden appearance. Then his eyes moved from Loke to me and back again.

"We were waiting up for my grandmother," I said, desperately wishing that my cheeks wouldn't flame so hotly at thoughts that hadn't even been spoken aloud. "That's why we're still wearing yester-day's clothes. And I'm sure my hair is doing something rather interest-ing," I added mostly to myself. I touched the back of my head and did indeed find an impressive tangle just where it had been resting on the back of the sofa.

"It doesn't matter," Andrew said. "There's been a murder."

"Who?" I demanded, even as my head tried to come up with a quick list of possibilities. The first, chillingly, was my own still-absent grandmother. But I reminded myself that Andrew had come looking for her. He wouldn't do that if she had been the victim.

Still, the dark voices in my head were just *sure* that this was related to the rest of the troubles. It had to be someone with magic, right? A death that had affected the spells.

"Oh no," I said, pressing trembling fingertips to my mouth. "Not Kara."

"Kara?" Loke repeated, confused but also concerned. As usual, he followed my mental processes faster than anyone. "Not Kara," he agreed. But he looked to Andrew for confirmation.

"What? Kara? No," he said, his words all in a tumble. "Why would you think it was Kara?"

"Never mind. Who was it?" I asked.

"I don't think you know him. His name was Dave Miller. He went to high school a couple of years behind Michelle, Jessica and I, but he's been living somewhere else pretty much ever since. He's only recently back in town," Andrew said.

I exchanged a look with Loke, and I could see my own relief reflected in his eyes. Whatever this was, it wasn't about the spells. And as horrific as any murder was, getting to the bottom of one was just something I did on a far too regular basis.

"I don't understand why this is so upsetting to you," Loke said.

"You do look like you're about to jump out of your own skin," I agreed. "Was he a friend of yours?"

"I barely knew the guy," Andrew said. "No, it's Jessica."

"Jessica has been hurt?" I asked as all those familiar panic feelings started building inside me all over again.

"She's been arrested," Andrew said. "Dave was found dead in the basement of her café, with one of her knives buried between his shoulder blades. He was stabbed from behind, then pushed down a flight of stairs and left there on the basement floor to bleed out."

"And they think Jessica did this?" I said, incredulous.

"Surely they only picked her up to ask her questions," Loke said reasonably. "They can't really believe she killed this man just because a knife she uses daily inside her own café was used to murder him, again inside her own café. What would her motive possibly be?"

"I don't know. I don't know," Andrew said, raking his hands through his hair. "The officer I spoke to didn't make much sense."

"Or you couldn't hear much sense," I said as kindly as I could. "You look very shaken up. You might not have been hearing what he was saying properly."

"Maybe. Maybe," he said, still tearing at his hair. Then he gave me an imploring look. "Where did Nora go? No slight to you, but she's been speaking for the people of this community for decades now. I really need her to help me explain things to the police. I tried, but..." He trailed off, lifting his hands in the air helplessly.

"She went inside the hall," Loke said. "Maybe we should check on her. For a couple of reasons."

He gave me a significant look, but I just tugged at my bottom lip as I mulled it over.

She had been very clear she didn't want to be disturbed. But she had said nothing about being gone for hours and hours. At what point would she not be angry with me for being worried enough to go in after her?

Knowing my grandmother, that point was probably days in the future. If ever.

But I wasn't prepared to let it go so long. As horrible as this new murder was, it at least provided a handy excuse to intrude on her and whatever she was doing.

Finally, I nodded to Loke. "Let's do it. The worst she can do is chew me out."

The three of us crossed the parking lot to the main door to the hall. It was cold stainless steel now, if recently painted. I could feel the spells lurking just beyond it, still pulsating at their full strength, but the illusions that made the building look like a Viking-era long house never affected this particular vantage point.

I wasn't entirely surprised to find the door barred. I knocked, as loudly as I could. When that received no answer, Loke tried knocking quite a bit louder than I had managed. But still, there was no answer.

"Can you magic your way in there?" Loke asked me.

"No more than you can," I said to him in a low voice. But Andrew didn't really seem to be listening to me. He was standing back a few feet, his body so tense with anxiety he was practically vibrating in place.

"Where's Michelle?" I asked him.

He gave me a startled look that morphed into one of chagrin. "I don't think she knows yet."

"So, you were there with Jessica when she was picked up?" Loke asked.

"My grandfather saw the police cars pull up from where he was behind the counter in the service station. I was upstairs in my shop, but he called me down just as Jessica came walking up the road to open the café for the day," he said.

"So she wasn't the one who found the body?" I asked.

"I don't think so. I don't know who did. I don't know anything." He ground out that last with a lot of self-recrimination.

Which wasn't exactly helpful now. "There will be time enough later for all of us to vent our frustrations, but right now we need to focus," I said.

"Right," Andrew said, nodding briskly. "Nora?"

I sighed. "You're not the only one frustrated by a lack of knowledge. But, like I said, now's not the time. For the moment, it's just the three of us. But we've got this, right? We've been here before."

"I'm going to leave your grandmother a note in her trailer so if she comes out while we're gone, she'll know where we went," Loke said.

"Thank you," I said. He gave me a curt nod, then crossed the parking lot back towards the trailer.

"What do we do first?" Andrew asked. "Examine the crime scene? You can do your drawing thing?" But before I could say a word, he was vehemently shaking his head. "No. No, the first thing has to be to go see Jessica. I can only imagine what she's going through right now."

"She's being questioned by police, but we don't know if she's actually a suspect," I said.

"They put her in cuffs," he said in a hissing voice, as if the very memory of it sickened him.

"Right. That sounds like she's a suspect," I gave in with a sigh. "Well, even so. We know she didn't do it. They will too, soon enough. As frustrating as it is that it looks like they may be losing valuable time chasing the wrong lead, there's not much we can do about that. Not until we know more."

"So what happens now?" he asked.

"Now, I'm guessing Jessica is getting her court-appointed lawyer, and she's not saying a word until she has one," I said.

I really hoped that was true. Jessica always struck me as being very level-headed. But she'd never been accused of murder before. That could knock anyone off balance.

"I meant what do we do now?" he said.

There was a loud bang, the door to the trailer home once more swinging too quickly open. I looked over as Loke caught it then closed it more carefully than he had opened it.

"The first thing we should do is talk to Michelle," I said. "She was also right across the street, so she probably knows already."

I didn't add that Michelle likely knew more than even Andrew did at this point. I could so clearly see a panicked Andrew running out of the service station as Jessica was packed into the back of a squad car. I could see him demanding answers from an officer who may have had his hands full with other tasks at the time. Or he may have answered all of Andrew's questions as fully as he could; I didn't know.

What I *did* know was that Andrew was still visibly squirrelly. I doubted he was holding information well at the moment. If Michelle was holding up like her usual self, her brain would be processing better.

Alternatively, she hadn't run down to find Nora or me straight away. She might still be gathering information from the other officers on the scene.

Either way, we had to talk to her first. She was Jessica's best friend. I didn't even want to start coming up with a plan until Michelle was on board to help.

"Let's talk to Michelle," Andrew agreed. That plan of action seemed to calm his nerves a little. Or just having any plan of action at all might have done that.

But as we climbed the path up the steep bluffs to the crossroads, I looked back down at the meeting hall behind us. I could see the dance of magic better from this angle than standing right before its most mundane doors.

It looked just as it always did to me, since I had learned to see things in the magical world. But somehow that was no comfort at all. I almost wished it looked like a black hole or a cyclone of energy or some malevolent all-seeing eye.

Anything but what it was: the spells my grandmother and I were most familiar with in all the worlds we knew. Now turned against us.

CHAPTER TEN

WHEN THE THREE of us arrived at the restaurant, the cooler, air-conditioned interior greeted us with the smell of cooking eggs, bacon and sausage, with undertones of pancakes and waffles, and of course their signature item: fresh hash browns cooked to crispy, creamy perfection.

My stomach growled. But work came first.

I blinked to adjust my eyes after leaving behind the bright mid June sun, then found Michelle standing close to her mother Anna as they talked together by the window to the kitchen. Michelle's honey blonde hair was pulled up in a ponytail as it always was when she was working. Her mother's silvery blonde hair was up in the same style. If not for that touch of gray to her hair, the two could pass as sisters, so Michelle had some nice genetics for slow aging to look forward to.

The cook set a couple of plates of steaming bacon and eggs on the window counter, and Anna took them both while giving Michelle a quick nod. Then she went to take them to a table in the back of the restaurant while Michelle fast-walked across the restaurant to pull Andrew into a tight hug.

"It's going to be all right," she assured him. "We've got this, right?"

"Right," he mumbled, but didn't step out of her hug.

Loke and I were barely inside the doors. I guessed he felt like I did, that moving further into the restaurant would be intruding somehow. But I had never seen my Runde friends so distraught before.

I gave Loke a questioning look. He had, after all, known them all longer than I had. When I came to town, he had been living a dual life, Loke in Villmark and Luke in Runde. I was sure most of Runde still knew him as Luke, but Michelle, Andrew and Jessica had learned the truth about him and Villmark months ago.

To my surprise, Loke answered my look with a smirk. It was a smirk he quickly wiped away with his hand, then schooled his face into a more stern look, but I knew what I had seen. Something was amusing him. Despite everything going on, he still had the capacity for inappropriate sources of humor.

It was almost enough to make me smile as well.

Almost.

"Right," Michelle said at last, and Andrew took the hint and stepped back from her. Then she gave me a quick hug and Loke an acknowledging nod of hello. "The breakfast rush is winding down, so I can take a few minutes here before we have to start gearing up for lunch. Let's grab a booth."

We followed her to the far side of the restaurant towards one of the larger corner booths. As I passed the long counter where single diners usually ate, I saw a now-familiar head of curly brown hair. It was the guy I had collided with the night before.

The man in question was just getting up, digging into the pocket of his jeans for cash to pay his bill. He saw me looking at him and gave me a nod of recognition, then set his money next to his empty plate and headed out the door.

I eyed the money in passing: a ten and a five. For coffee and a two-two-two? So he was a good tipper, anyway.

I hurried to join the others just as Anna brought a tray of mugs and a carafe of coffee and distributed them out. She gave Andrew's shoulder an encouraging squeeze before bustling away again.

"What do you know?" I asked without preamble. Time was short, after all. And the idea of drinking yet more coffee was positively stomach-churning.

But I had some anyway. I was going to need the caffeine.

"Jessica is a person of interest at this point, not a suspect," she said, and Andrew slumped back against the back of his seat in palpable relief.

"She should still get a lawyer, though," I said.

"She has one," Michelle assured me. "Or at least she's arranged to meet with one. My mom sent one of our regulars to the station to give her some names to call."

"What happened?" Loke asked. "I don't even know this Dave fellow, whoever he is."

"No, I don't suppose you would," Michelle said. "He went to high school with the rest of us, back in the day. But he's only recently come back to town." She looked over at Andrew, who nodded in mute agreement.

"Is high school relevant now, though?" I asked.

"Sadly, I think so," Michelle said. She poured herself a cup of coffee but only wrapped her hands around it as if for warmth, not taking a sip. "Dave was at the mead hall last night, briefly. Don't you remember?"

"No," I said, and looked at Loke.

"Is he the fellow who came in and then went straight out again?" he asked Michelle. "The one who upset what's-her-name so much?"

"Heather Peterson, yes," Michelle agreed.

"Oh, I remember that moment. But I just missed seeing him," I said. I felt a flare of frustration for a missed opportunity. What would I have seen if I had caught a glimpse of him hours before his murder? Probably nothing. If I wasn't actively looking into the magical world, I tended not to see things like premonitions or signs. It wasn't like I was a valkyrie who could see when someone was marked for imminent death or anything.

Although that would really be handy if I could.

"Jessica gave him her death glare, and he scurried right back out of there," Michelle said, sounding proud of her friend.

"Jessica has a death glare?" I asked.

"Totally," Andrew said. He was toying with his coffee cup, not looking up at me, but he sounded proud of her as well.

"She only unleashes it when it's really warranted, but you definitely don't want to be on the receiving end of that," Michelle said with a short, humorless laugh.

"That's probably not good," Loke said. "If anyone in the mead hall saw her doing that to someone who turned up dead the next morning, it's no wonder she's a suspect."

"Person of interest," Michelle corrected him. "And that's mainly because the murder was committed inside her café with a knife that will surely be covered in her fingerprints when it comes back from the crime lab."

"Still, Loke's not wrong," I said. "But let's back up. Why was she shooting death glares at this Dave person?"

"She was protecting Heather," Andrew said, still focused on the handle of his coffee cup.

"From Dave?" I asked.

"Yeah," Michelle said. "Heather came back into town a few weeks ago, but she was only here for a few days before Dave was back in town, too."

"I'm guessing not a coincidence?" I said.

"That I don't know," Michelle said. "But he was definitely trying to talk to her once he was here."

"Like in a stalker kind of way?" I asked.

"Pretty much," Michelle said. Then she bit down hard on her bottom lip and although her eyes showed no hint of wetness, I could tell she was fighting back tears. "This is where I feel like the worst kind of friend, leaving Jessica alone to deal with this."

"You weren't the only one who wasn't there," Andrew said in a thick voice.

"Come on, you guys. If Jessica thought there was any real danger, she would've come to all of us for help. She's not the wait to be rescued type," I said sternly. Although I was feeling like a neglectful friend myself.

"Jessica felt like she had everything under control," Loke put in. "She said so just last night. She might've been wrong, but she wasn't lying. You took her at her word. No need to beat yourselves up about it."

Neither Andrew nor Michelle answered. They just stared gloomily down at their coffee.

"So Jessica was helping out Heather, and Heather had a stalker problem," I said, "or Jessica was helping out Heather *because* she had a stalker problem?"

"Honestly, I don't know which," Michelle said. "Or why she put herself out like she did. We weren't talking enough before this all happened. Not that we weren't *talking*, but..." she broke off when her voice started to crack, and I all but lunged across the table to squeeze her hand.

"We talked about this just last night, so you know I'm not judging you," I said. "I just need to know more about this Dave fellow. And Heather too. Maybe we can start with why Heather wasn't picked up, too. Doesn't she work in the café? Doesn't she have access to all the same knives Jessica does?"

"I don't know if she was picked up or not, actually," Michelle said. Andrew looked up from his coffee long enough to meet her eyes and shake his head. He didn't know either.

"We can go looking for her, I guess," Loke suggested.

"We'll put it on the list," I said. "What else can you tell me about Dave?"

"He was banned from the café, actually," Michelle said. "Since about a week ago. You know about that day, right?" she said to Andrew.

Andrew, slumped back in his seat, just nodded mutely.

"What happened?" I asked.

"I don't know the beginning of the story," Michelle said.

"We really need to talk to Jessica," Andrew put in under his breath.

"Tell me about it," she agreed. "But anyway, I guess Dave came around one time too many to try to see Heather while she was working in the café. And Jessica chased him out into the parking lot. She banned him from the property, is the long and the short of it. And as far as I know, he never went back. Only, I guess, maybe this morning he did."

"There was a lot of shouting, apparently," Andrew said, still sitting with his arms crossed and glaring at his untouched cup of coffee. "She was angry. And a lot of people saw her. Like what Loke said about the death glare in the mead hall."

"We were in the shadows. It's possible no one saw that but a few of us," Michelle said.

Andrew shrugged, unconvinced but not willing to argue.

I blew out a long breath. "So these two dated in high school or what? Did she leave town to avoid him? In which case, why did she come back?"

"Again, I have to regret how little I've been communicating with Jessica," Michelle said. "I just don't know." Then something caught the corner of her eye and she turned, then gave a little wave to her mother. "And I'm about out of time here."

"We have enough to start with, anyway," I told her. "And we'll be back to catch you up on what we learn when we learn it."

"I know you will. I feel better just knowing you're here with us and on the case," Michelle said. Then she slid out of the booth. I got up to give her one last hug, then sat back down.

Andrew hadn't moved a muscle. He was still glaring down at his coffee cup as if he blamed it for everything. But I could see all the tension was back in his body. The little muscle in his jaw was spasming even as I looked at it.

"What's first, then?" Loke asked. "Finding Heather?"

"I suppose that ought to be the top item," I said.

"Only you want to do something else first," Loke guessed.

"I do," I admitted. "Only it's going to be tricky if the police are still there."

"You want to draw the crime scene," Loke said. Then he grinned, that old familiar grin of his.

Trust Loke to be tickled with the idea of sneaking past a police barricade in the middle of the day.

"It's where I get the best clues," I said simply. "I just feel like we should start there."

"I'm game," Loke said. As if I even needed him to say it out loud.

We both got out of the booth. But I realized that Andrew hadn't moved to follow us, and I turned back.

"Andrew? Did you want to stay here?" I asked.

"No, I'll go with you guys," he said. He slid out of the booth, but he still wasn't quite meeting my eyes.

"Or did you want to split up? Do you want to look for Heather while Loke and I potentially risk breaking the law?" I asked.

"Or did you want to go to the police station and check in on Jessica?" Loke asked.

"No, they won't let me see her until she's released, and then she'll be right back here anyway," he said woodenly.

I gave Loke another questioning look. Because Andrew's answer had come far too quickly. Clearly, he knew what he said was a fact because it was the one thing he could reliably remember from what the police officer on the scene had told him.

Loke didn't grin at me this time, but I could still see mischief in his eyes.

But all he said was, "Or do you think we should make another try at getting Nora's attention?"

"No, let's just do your thing," Andrew said. His enthusiasm for what he was saying would need to be measured on a scale with negative numbers.

"Are you sure?" I asked.

He finally looked up at me, and the sad frustration in his red-rimmed eyes was so powerful I found myself staggering back half a step. Loke's hand on my shoulder stopped me from stumbling back to awkwardly fall into the booth behind me.

"I'm sure," Andrew said. "Let's just do this. Let's clear Jessica's name."

I nodded, then led the way out of the restaurant, back out into the midmorning of a perfect June day.

But even when the warmth of the sun hit me full in the face, my insides felt icy cold.

There was something Andrew wasn't telling me. And there was a lot I didn't know about just what had happened back in everyone's high school days that had triggered all of these current events.

I could only hope that the guilt wracking Andrew was the same as the guilt wracking Michelle. He was working as an EMT part-time, with his grandfather part-time, and on top of that was constantly building boats and furniture in his workshop. Perhaps lately he had had as little time for Jessica as Michelle had had, and the overlap of that was making both of them feel twice as bad.

But I couldn't shake the feeling that something else was bothering him. Had he played some other, deeper role in this whole drama, maybe back in high school?

I would ask him, but I really didn't want to have that conversation in front of the always-laughing Loke.

Besides that, I had meant what I said, that I wanted to examine the crime scene first. All the other leads would make more sense to me after I had that scene firmly in my mind.

All I had to do was find a way to get a few undisturbed minutes on the far side of the police tape.

And keep tuning out my fears about my grandmother, and the mead hall, and Villmark.

One of those things was far harder than the other. But I gritted my teeth and set about doing both.

CHAPTER ELEVEN

WE CROSSED the highway from the restaurant to the café, always a hairy proposition given the number of trucks that used this road and the lack of a clearly marked crosswalk. Runde was barely a dot on the maps, and—save for these three buildings clustered close to the freeway—was out of sight down in the valley under the overpass.

Out of sight, out of mind.

The restaurant did a good business between the truckers who made a point of stopping there and the tourists who flocked all the way up and down the North Shore, especially in June. I admit I wasn't entirely sure how Andrew's grandfather kept the gas station in business. I rarely saw anyone at the pumps. But he was the best mechanic in the area, so he had that going for him.

Jessica's café was the newest addition to the cluster by the highway. I had no idea what it had been before she had acquired it, but she had been just preparing to open up the day I came into town nearly nine months before. Every time I had been back since, she had been doing a brisk business with tourists and locals both.

Her shop's Wi-Fi was markedly better than anything available down in Runde. There were places throughout the valley by the lake shore where phones couldn't grab a connection, and all the homes still had dial-up modems. The internet part of her café was a huge draw, especially in the first few weeks.

But then people started browsing her carefully selected offering of books, and her fine baked goods and hot beverages.

And a few even bought the work from local artists that she displayed throughout the café, including a lot of my own pen and ink work. In fact, that was the only thing keeping my bank account in the black these days.

Being a volva wasn't a paying gig. But it was definitely a more than full-time one.

I tried hard not to dwell on it, because it was a deeply selfish thought, but I couldn't push away the fear that if anything happened with Jessica and her café, I would have no income at all.

"What are we going to do?" Loke asked me as the three of us made it successfully across the highway and stood at the very edge of Jessica's parking lot. At first I was confused as to what he was talking about, but then I saw there was still a single police car parked near the front door. And I could make out the outlines of at least two officers inside.

"We could wait for them to leave," Andrew suggested. "They can't stay here all day. They don't have the shift coverage for that these days. Budget cuts," he added for my benefit.

"I'm not a big fan of waiting," I said. Although I had no better idea.

"Have you ever been down to the basement?" Loke asked. I shook my head. I hadn't even known there *was* a basement.

"I have," Andrew said. "Jessica uses it for storage. There's also a washing machine and dryer down there she uses for the linens and towels."

"It's built right into the side of the bluff. Is it a walkout basement? Any sort of back door?" Loke asked.

Andrew frowned as he searched his memory. "There isn't a back door. There are a few windows, but they're very high up and quite small. Maybe Ingrid could squeeze through one of them?"

"Not without risking being seen," I said. "Is the only door anywhere in the basement the one at the top of the stairs?"

"I mean, the laundry room is separate from the rest of the storage space. There's a door there," Andrew said.

"Do you have to have seen a door to use it?" I asked Loke.

He laughed out loud. "Man, how much simpler would my life be if *that* were true?"

"What are we talking about?" Andrew asked.

"You said you could still get around Runde, right?" I asked Loke, ignoring Andrew for the moment.

"When I tested it, that was true," he said with a shrug. "Apparently, these things can change without warning, so no promises."

"But if you were to walk in through the door to the shed at the bottom of the property, you could come out inside the basement?" I asked.

"There's a shed?" Loke said.

"It's hidden in the overgrown shrubs and weeds at the very edge of the bluff," Andrew said. "Ironically, it's filled with landscaping equipment."

"Can it be seen from inside the café?" I asked.

"Not if we come at it from the south side," Andrew said.

"Lead the way, then," Loke said, cracking his knuckles. "I'll handle the rest."

We swished through overly-tall grass, walking as close as possible to the scratchy bushes that grew just before the point where the bluff dropped off steeply down to Runde proper below. The shed wasn't hard to spot, even faded as it was by the years of sunlight that had worn away most of its paint. But it was hidden from view of the café itself by tall tangles of brambles and weeds.

Not that it was likely that the officers within were gazing out the windows. But better safe than sorry.

"You got this," I said to Loke as he reached for the door handle.

"I still don't understand—" Andrew started to say, when Loke pushed the door open with a flourish and disappeared inside. I took Andrew by the arm and pulled him with me to follow Loke.

And just like that, we were standing on the hard dirt floor of the café basement. I turned back to see nothing behind me but the darkened interior of an unlit laundry room. The washing machine and dryer both looked like they'd seen better days. And those days were when colors like harvest gold and avocado green struck anyone as being a good idea. But judging from the stacks of neatly folded aprons, napkins and towels, they functioned well enough.

"What just happened?" Andrew asked, rubbing at his head.

"Just a touch of magic," I said with a reassuring smile. "Not mine this time, though."

"It's a bit of a jolt the first time," Loke said sympathetically.

"So it gets easier?" Andrew said.

"Well, no," Loke said, and unfurled his grin at both of us.

"Come on. I need to look around," I said, and headed for the far end of the basement, to the bottom of the stairs.

I didn't quite reach it. The body was gone, but it wasn't hard to tell where it had been. Not only were there still numbered markers identifying where objects had been taken as evidence after being photographed, the dirt itself was stickily soaked with blood.

"Okay, I'm just going to do a quick drawing," I said to the other two in a low whisper. We could hear the creaking of the floorboards every time one of the officers overhead took a step, but our own moving around was relatively silent thanks to the dusty floor.

I sat down on the surprisingly cold ground. It might be a warm June day outside, but inside this basement, it was still cool enough to store food if one were so inclined. I took out my sketchbook, hurriedly turned past the drawing of Esja sleeping in the chair while Loke was busy trying to see out the very dirty windows in the back, and grabbed my pencils.

"Is there anything I can do to help? Anything at all?" Andrew asked. His voice was choked, almost anguished, but in the semidarkness of the basement I couldn't quite see his face.

"You already helped by showing us the shed," I told him. "And I know you'll be helping again as soon as we're done here. But, sorry, the next few minutes I have to do this alone."

"Right," he said, and took several steps back. Loke caught him by the arm and drew him further away. As if the dirt-encrusted windows were so fascinating.

I took a breath, cleared my mind, and started to draw. I was just thinking how things were so much easier for me now than they had been just months before when I looked down at my work and saw nothing but Xs all over the page.

My pencil tip snapped at the same moment. With a sigh, I turned to a new page and took out a fresh pencil.

This sort of thing happened all the time when I started working with a new rune. I had been meant to be meditating on it already, but the events of the night before and the morning so far had made that quite impossible.

But clearly the gipt rune had no sympathy for my problems. It was ready to speak to me, so speak to me it would.

I took three deep breaths this time, made extra sure I had cleared my mind, and only then set the pencil to paper.

The next minutes went by in one long instant, and when I finally opened my eyes and focused on the page before me, I could see a single sketch done in incredible detail.

There was a man sprawled just where the markers on the ground before me said he should be. I could see the knife between his shoulder blades. It was a small blade, and I had a phantom sensation of smelling vanilla even more strongly than I smelled the coppery smell of the blood that was soaking the dirt floor.

Jessica used fresh vanilla beans whenever she wanted to add vanilla flavor to anything. Never extract. I suspected the small blade in my drawing had been used for that purpose. For scraping out seeds from inside a vanilla bean.

Such a blade was far too short to kill a man, particularly not a man of the larger than average size I saw in my sketch. No, it was the tumble down the stairs that had done that. The knife had just been to distract him. Or to draw his attention. One or the other.

I glanced up at the staircase. It was in the deepest shadowy corner of the basement, furthest from the dingy light filtering in through the sparse windows. But I could see the bright white of the numbered marker cards on nearly all the stairs. He had hit hard enough to leave a mark or even blood in all those places.

I looked down at my drawing again. There was a figure, or rather the outline of a figure, looking down from the open doorway at the top of the stairs. Beyond her was white light, but she herself was in shadow. But her outline held many details. I could see the wisps of her hair hanging loosely, the folds of a loose-fitting shirt I suspected was flannel.

And the shape of another, longer knife in her right hand as her left hand grasped the doorway. She was leaning into the basement to look down the steps at her handiwork.

But she had never come down. She had seen enough from there to just walk away.

"Is that Jessica?" Andrew asked. He had appeared behind me so suddenly I jumped at his voice, even though he was still whispering.

"It looks like her, doesn't it?" I sighed. "Why did she change her hair? Do you know?"

"Does it matter?" Andrew asked. "It was a couple of weeks ago."

"Before or after Heather came to town?" I pressed.

He frowned in thought. "After?" he said. But he didn't sound sure.

"Jessica and Heather have the same hair now," Loke said, completely unnecessarily. He knew we were all thinking it, anyway. "It could be either one of them. Couldn't it?"

"Even if that is Jessica at the top of the stairs, there is nothing in that picture that means she did this. Maybe she heard something moving around down here and grabbed a knife to go check it out. Then she saw the body and just backed away," Andrew said.

I tapped my pencil on the sketchbook as I mulled it over, but I didn't like that theory at all.

"Nope. I don't buy it," I said as I put my things away and stood up.

"It's plausible," Andrew said.

"Not for Jessica, it isn't," I said as I dusted off the back of my jeans. "This isn't her first dead body, for one thing. So she's not going to be so shocked that she behaves out of character. And fleeing the scene of a crime without reporting it to anybody is definitely out of character."

Andrew blew out a frustrated breath, but nodded. "You're right. She wouldn't do that. She didn't call the cops. And she didn't call me. Or you. Or, I think we can safely say, Michelle. So, yeah. You're right. So where does that leave us?"

I looked towards the door at the top of the stairs. "I really wish I could draw upstairs. That's where everything happened. All I get from this is where the body was. And that someone, Jessica or Heather, was looking down from above. But whatever altercation there was, it didn't happen here. It happened up there."

"And yet," Loke said, and pointed to the unfinished ceiling above us. As if on cue, one of the police officers walked by again, the floorboards creaking loudly at their passage.

"Maybe later, then," I said. But my frustration was making me feel almost ill.

Or maybe that was all the coffee and no food. I should really start keeping a protein bar or two in my art bag.

"Should we look for Heather now?" Andrew asked.

"No, not yet," I said. "We will, but there's one more thing I want to check first."

"What's that?" Loke asked.

"Do you know where Dave was staying? I'm not getting any kind of read on him from what I drew here, because he was most likely dead before he got here. With upstairs not being an option yet, I would like to see his personal space. If that's even remotely possible," I said.

Andrew chewed at his lip but shook his head. "I don't, but I'm sure someone does. Give me a second to text everyone I know. Then we can start walking down to Runde. We're bound to have an answer before we even get down to the lake."

Loke was already waiting at the now-closed door to the laundry room. I walked over to him, Andrew trailing behind me as he walked and typed on his phone at the same time.

Good thing we were on the top of the bluff. Best Wi-Fi or cell coverage in Runde. I just hoped whoever he was texting was having as good of a connection.

We followed Loke through the door and out into the overgrown yard by the landscaping shed.

CHAPTER TWELVE

As the three of us walked away from the highway, following the narrow footpath that cut across the switchback road that brought cars in and out of Runde, I was finding it a little hard to focus on the case at hand.

Part of that was worry about my grandmother. We still hadn't heard from her. If the lead we were currently following brought us close to the meeting hall, I was definitely going to try really quickly to get inside again. Or at least check the trailer home to see if it looked like she'd been there since we left.

How long could it take to get to the bottom of some spells?

I actually had no idea. I had never tried to undo that sort of work. I had never even tried to *do* that sort of work. I had only ever assisted her with such things.

But it really felt like too much time had passed without hearing from her. I couldn't imagine what sort of danger could find her, safe within the walls of her sacred space. The mead hall was her masterwork, what she had put all of her energy in for decades after, I didn't really know how many decades she had spent learning how to do it all.

A lot, anyway. My grandmother was older than she looked. And she had packed a lot of work into each of those decades.

Yes, something had turned on us. But I just couldn't bring myself to believe it had turned on us so badly as all that. It was a glitch, not a catastrophe.

And being too busy to remember to check in was exactly the sort of thing my grandmother would do, anyway. She was busy fixing the glitch. That was all.

Or so I fiercely hoped.

So, as we walked, my thoughts were preoccupied. I think that would be fair to say.

Andrew also seemed preoccupied, but to my shame, I was pretty sure his only thoughts were of Jessica and how to help her get out of this strange jam. Just where my thoughts should be.

Loke, for his part, was clearly still deeply amused by something. He kept looking at Andrew, then at me, then at Andrew again. I was tempted to demand to know what was so very funny in this most inappropriate of moments.

But then I remembered Esja. If worry for her wasn't totally consuming him, it was only because he'd found this mysterious source of amusement to focus on. He needed that focus. Calling him out on being inappropriately amused was not going to be helpful to his outlook.

And I might need his help again to solve this case. Or to get us all back to Villmark. So let him enjoy his private jokes.

I heard something buzzing, then Andrew pulled his phone out of his back pocket. We had reached the bottom of the path, the lake now filling the eastern horizon directly in front of us, so we all stopped while he checked his texts.

"Okay, he's staying in the apartment of the garage at Owen Sorensen's place," he said as he tucked the phone back into his pocket.

"Owen Sorensen," I said, but even saying it aloud jogged no memories in me. "Is he a fishing Sorensen or a farming Sorensen?"

"Fishing," Andrew said. "He's two houses down from my grandfather's place, actually. Just up ahead on the lake shore south of here."

"Short walk then," I said cheerily. But inside, my heart sank a little.

We weren't going to be going past the meeting hall after all. Checking up on my grandmother would have to wait for another time.

"Tell me about Dave," I said to Andrew as we walked along the shoulder of the unevenly paved road. "I didn't see him when he was at the mead hall last night, but from my sketch, he looked like a big guy. Football player, maybe?"

"Not that I recall," Andrew said. "He was three years behind me, maybe four? I'm not sure. I barely remember him. People on the group text are saying some things that are bringing details back, but my own memory is pretty murky. But he definitely wasn't an athlete."

"Are you sure?" I asked. Michelle would probably remember more. I made a mental note to ask her when we got back to the restaurant.

"Yeah, now that I'm thinking about it, he was like our high school's big math star," Andrew said.

"Your high school had a math star?" Loke asked, half amused and half confused.

"You know what I mean," Andrew said to me.

"I think my high school was easily ten times the size of yours, but yeah, I know what you're getting at," I said. "Scored super high on the SATs. Always placed in the science fair competitions. That sort of thing?"

"Yeah, but he wasn't so much a science or engineering guy as just straight math," Andrew said. "He did a lot of tutoring. Because of that, he looked like he was always hanging out with the jocks. But they just needed him to pass their classes. He was tall and wide, sure enough, but not remotely athletic."

"So big but soft, like a teddy bear," I said.

"With glasses," Andrew said.

Of course, in my sketch of him, he had been facedown. With that little knife in his back. And the flannel shirt he had been wearing had billowed around him, not really revealing any of the outlines of his body. But soft felt right. Not fat, just not a body that ever worked out.

And I supposed one of those little evidence markers numbered the location where his glasses had fallen. But I didn't want to think about that. It was all too real then. It made him too human. Better if he was just a victim that only existed on paper. It made it easier for me to focus on finding clues.

"So he left Runde on a scholarship after high school, I'm guessing?" I said. "He's three years behind you, which makes him…"

"Too young to be done with college yet, yes," Andrew agreed, although my mental math hadn't taken me that far yet.

"Dropped out? Or taking a break?" I pondered.

"Or got early release because he's a math star," Loke put in.

"I'm not sure. I really didn't know him at all. I only remember this much because of the chatter on the group text. Sorry," Andrew finished.

"It's a start," I said. "And I'm guessing Michelle is on your group text. Whatever she and her mother don't know about anyone from Runde, they can find out by this afternoon. And I'm sure they're working on that already."

"You're not wrong," Andrew agreed. He sounded ever so slightly cheered by that.

We reached the end of a long driveway flanked by evergreen trees and turned up it until we reached a modest one-story house on the shoreline. There was a fish house built right on the water behind it, and the driveway itself ended in a detached garage.

That garage didn't look tall enough to have an apartment on top of it. I supposed you could just barely cram a little space under the eaves of its peaked roof, maybe. But I couldn't imagine someone the size of Dave Miller squeezing in there.

As we approached, our feet crunching loudly on the gravel of the driveway, the front door of the little house opened and an older man in faded jeans and an even more faded Twins baseball jersey stepped out onto the concrete steps that led down to his front walk.

"Can I help you?" he asked, in a far stronger Runde accent than any of my friends sported. Purely northern Minnesotan, it was the sort of cadence where you knew at once this person was never going to talk faster no matter how much you tried to rush them.

I took a deep breath and summoned all my conversational patience.

"We were looking for Dave Miller," I said. "Or rather, where he lives. Lived. I guess you know what happened?" I finished lamely.

"Yah," Owen said. And that was it. Then his gaze just drifted off of the three of us, towards the sparkling waters of Lake Superior off to his right.

"I'm sorry, I should've introduced myself first. I'm Ingrid Torfa, Nora's granddaughter," I said. I even touched my own chest, as if there could be any confusion as to who I was referring to.

But he just said, "Yah," again. Still looking out at the lake.

"You rented him a room?" I asked.

"Oh, sure," he said, nodding as if to himself. "Well, only for the month, though. Only for the month." It took him forever to get all those words out. Which was all the more maddening for being the same thing twice, with a little unnecessary filler sprinkled in.

I took another deep breath. "May we see it?" I asked.

"The police have already been by," he said. "But I reckon if you just want to take a look at it, I don't see the harm in that. The stairs are up the back there."

"Thank you, Mr. Sorensen," I said, and hustled Andrew and Loke with me to the back of the garage.

And I had thought the stairs in the café basement had looked narrow and dangerously steep. These were that, but also barely attached to the back wall of the garage. And that wall had a definite outward slope. Like the whole building was only waiting for one last November gale to collapse to a pile of concrete blocks and rubble.

The police had left crime scene tape across the outside of the door, but the door itself was unlocked and swung inward when I turned the knob. I ducked under the tape and stepped inside.

The whole space smelled both of gas fumes and cut grass. I guessed Mr. Sorensen spent more time on his riding mower than in his car these days. Well, his long, narrow yard had indeed looked lovingly maintained.

"What are we even looking for?" Andrew asked from the doorway.

"You guys don't need to come in," I said. "I just need to get a feel of the place, really. If there were any real clues, the police would have them already."

"Come on. Let's get off these stairs. The whole place feels like a death trap," Loke mumbled to Andrew. Then Andrew's outline was gone from the open doorway and I was momentarily alone.

I looked down at the narrow camp bed, neatly made. There was a footlocker beside it, but that had clearly been thoroughly rifled through, clothes in disarray and anything remotely interesting defi- nitely long gone. There was a shelf nearby that may have recently held a number of books, to judge from the marks in the dust that were all that remained.

But there was barely enough room for me to stand inside that room. Someone Dave's size, just by necessity, would only be coming up here to sleep.

So where had he been spending his days? And what had he been spending them doing?

Looking for work? Or just stalking Heather?

I sat down on the floor and whipped out my sketchbook. This time I used charcoals, working fast and dirty. I ended up with four sketches of different views of the space. Not as it was now, but as it had been when Dave had still lived in it.

The books appeared, but not their titles. And at some point, there had been a backpack, or maybe a computer bag, sitting next to the door. But there was nothing there now. Not even an outline in the dust.

No physical form of Dave emerged in my drawing, maybe because I still didn't know what he looked like. I wasn't sure what that meant, if anything. But I did *feel* him. Almost.

I turned a page and changed out the charcoal for ink pens. I used ink for my art all the time, but this was the first time I had ever felt like reaching for those pens to do my magic. But I didn't question the impulse. I just pulled off the cap, set the nib to paper, and let the drawing just happen.

By the time I was done, I had ink all over my fingers and a page full of dense detail. The ink on my fingers I was all too used to. Even using a contained pen and not a dip well or fountain pen, I still managed to make a mess I never noticed when caught up in the process. So that wasn't worrying.

The picture wasn't worrying either. It was just Dave alone, sprawled out on top of the narrow bed with an arm thrown over his eyes. And yet I could feel so many emotions radiating out of the drawing, in the stillness of that image.

He had been a stoic. Not in the sense of suppressing his emotions or somehow pulling off the trick of never having them in the first place. No, in the original sense of the word, of someone who feels feelings but remains a master of them.

He had loved Heather, in his own way. Which wasn't a possessive way. He wanted to see her healthy and thriving in the world, whether that was at his side or not.

And I could feel his worry over her, although I didn't quite understand it. Something about her troubled him. That was all I could tell.

But also he was distracted by something else. Something even vaguer.

Just why *had* he come back to town? Because somehow I didn't think it was really because Heather was there now.

I felt like I knew Dave pretty well now, even though we'd never met and I still had no idea what he looked like. But I was very sorry we had never met, because the man whose presence I had just felt had been a very decent fellow. He didn't deserve to be dead.

I gave my sketch one last look, and only then did I notice what should've jumped out at me at once. My crosshatching filled all the shadowy spaces in my drawing of the attic apartment, and there were many. And all that crosshatching was like the gipt rune everywhere. He had been surrounded by it.

Somehow, that just made my heart ache all the more. I didn't quite understand it, but it made me sad. It felt tied up in that love he had for Heather, and his worry for her, and how none of that had been remotely possessive.

Still lost in thought, I put my sketchbook away and climbed back down those rickety stairs. I rejoined Andrew and Loke, once more standing in awkward silence with Mr. Sorensen. Mr. Sorensen didn't seem to realize any of us were even there. It was like he had stepped out onto his front steps just to look at the lake. And he wasn't done looking at it just yet.

"Mr. Sorensen, can I ask you a few more questions?" I asked.

"Yah," he said. "Might not have answers, though."

"You didn't know Dave Miller well then?" I asked.

He chewed at something in his mouth. I didn't even want to guess at what was in there. But then he said merely, "Nope." And nothing more.

"How did you come to rent a room out to him?" I asked.

"Oh, I reckon," he said, then trailed off for so long I was afraid this was going to be the end of his sentence. But then he said, "Yah, it was Tore Nelsen's idea."

"Tore Nelsen knew Dave Miller, then?" I forced myself to ask.

I had dealt with Tore Nelsen before. The two men were about the same age, but Tore was even more eccentric than Owen Sorensen, if that were even possible. Definitely not someone I wanted to have to try talking to again. Owen may be slow in his answers, but Tore actively worked at not answering my questions.

But, "No, no," Owen said, annoyed at my misunderstanding. "It was Tore's idea to put something about that room on the internet. You know, like that website for letting people stay in your house. That was his idea."

"So Dave found you through a website?" I asked.

"Yeah," Owen said, jawing at whatever was in his mouth again. "Just needed the one room. Just for a month. But paid ahead of time. I've had spaghetti three times since. Haven't had spaghetti money in years."

Out of the corner of my eye, I saw Loke covering a smile with his hand and turning away. Andrew shot him a hard glare. But for his part, Owen Sorensen didn't seem to notice any of this.

I briefly wondered just what Owen ate on a regular basis that made spaghetti an extravagant treat. Probably a lot of fish he caught himself and canned food he got off the dented and expired shelf at a discount.

Best not to ask. I forced my mind back to the image of poor Dave Miller, face down in the café basement, a knife between his shoulder blades and his blood on every single step of those killer stairs.

"Do you know what Dave was doing while he was in town?" I asked.

"Not my business," Owen said sharply.

"No, of course not," I said, not quite sighing out loud. "Any visitors?" I tried instead.

"Nope," he said.

I traded glances with Andrew. Andrew rolled his eyes and shrugged. Neither of us thought anything useful was going to come out of this conversation. And it was getting past noon. Time to head back to the restaurant and catch Michelle at the end of the lunch rush.

"Well, thanks anyway, mister—" I started to say, when to my surprise Owen Sorensen just started monologuing.

"I was like him once, you know. Young and lost. That boy was definitely young and lost. Came into town to win back the girl, you know. The girl he'd loved in high school but left behind when he'd gone to the big city. Regretted that, he did. But I gather it was too late. Too little, too late, that's what they say, isn't it? Poor fella. Well, I was near fifty before I married myself, and barely seventy when I found myself a widower. So could be worse, is all I'm saying."

"You do realize Dave Miller is dead, right?" Loke said. The dark humor of it clearly tickled him.

I really wanted to kick him in the shin just then, but had to make do with a hard glare I knew he saw.

But Owen Sorensen chose that moment to turn away from the lake and pin his watery blue eyes sternly on Loke's face. "Yes, boy. I realize that. I know what I said."

Then he turned and went back into the house. The door slammed shut behind him, and then we heard the sound of a deadbolt being shot home.

"I'm not sure *that* was helpful," Andrew mumbled to me as we stood there stunned on the edge of his gravel driveway.

"Do we really want to assume Heather was the reason he came back to town?" I asked.

"I mean, has he even spoken with anyone else since he's been here?" Loke asked. "Besides our esteemed Mr. Owen Sorensen, of course."

"Yes," I said, hating myself for saying it. "He definitely spoke to Jessica."

"And we all know how that conversation ended," Andrew said.

"But we only have assumptions about where it *started*," I said. Then I blew out a sigh. "I suppose it was over Heather, like everyone says. What do you two think about Heather?"

"She's all right," Andrew said, not terribly helpfully.

I looked to Loke.

"She has a very chaotic energy," he said. Then he laughed. "And I should know."

"Chaotic how?" I asked.

"I can't tell who she is when I look at her. It's like there are too many overlapping images and I don't know which is the primary," he said.

I chewed at my lip, then realized Andrew was looking at both of us as if we were nuts.

"I'm sorry, but Heather has been triggering my paranoid instincts since I met her," I confessed. "I was worried she was going to be trouble for Jessica. But maybe I should've been taking a wider view."

"Honestly, I've probably spent the most time with her out of anyone besides Jessica, and I've never noticed any of that," Andrew said.

"Why so much time?" Loke asked casually.

Andrew flushed and looked away. "Well, I've been making deliveries to the café, and she's usually there with Jessica in the afternoons when I stop in. So. It's not a thing."

"Right," I said. His stammering nervousness was indicative of *something*, but just what it was, I'd have to work out later.

"So you don't trust Heather?" Loke said.

"I mean, all I do know is that Dave doesn't... didn't have stalker energy," I said. "He loved her truly and deeply, but not possessively. He was hopeful, but also pragmatic. Think everything that's the opposite of... say, Heathcliff from *Wuthering Heights*."

They both blinked at me, but neither wanted to admit they'd never read the book.

"I honestly don't remember Dave much at all," Andrew said. "Or Heather from back in high school, for that matter."

"Just because he loved her in the best sense of the word doesn't mean she was worthy of it," Loke pointed out.

"I know," I said. "Plus, I think there was something else going on. I really think the two of them turning up back in Runde after years away at pretty much the same time was just a coincidence."

"That would be a pretty big coincidence," Loke said.

"I know," I admitted. "Still, I think there's more going on than there seems to be. At least with Dave. Maybe with Heather too." Then I looked over at Andrew. "Get on your group text, will you? We need to find out where to find Heather."

"On it," Andrew said.

When we reached the end of the driveway, he turned back the way we'd come. I paused briefly in the middle of the road, peering westward through the trees to where I could just make out the outline of the back end of my grandmother's trailer home. The meeting hall was completely out of sight behind it.

I hoped she was doing all right. And that it wouldn't take too long to find Heather.

And that Heather would have the answers we needed.

CHAPTER THIRTEEN

WE WERE JUST CRUNCHING our way over the gravel parking lot in front of the closed café, about to cross the highway to the restaurant on the other side, when a blur of motion caught the corner of my eye. Andrew let out a woof of breath as a body collided with his in a fierce hug. At first I thought it was Jessica, what with the T-shirt emblazoned with the café logo and the loose blonde hair hanging past her shoulders. But then she pulled back enough to look Andrew in the face, and I saw the eerily over-blue eyes of Heather Peterson.

"Oh, Andrew! I've been looking for you everywhere!" she said, still holding on to him tightly. He patted her shoulder awkwardly, but she didn't take the hint to release him.

"We were just looking for you too," he said.

"Me? Why were you looking for me?" she asked. But she didn't wait for an answer, just plowed ahead with, "Isn't it terrible what happened? There's just no way Jessica did it. No way!"

"What do you know about what happened?" I asked.

She looked over at me as if startled to find me there. Then her eyes shifted from me to Loke, whose expression was unusually impassive. But then she was gazing up at Andrew again.

Couldn't she tell how uncomfortable she was making him? He

needed way more personal space than she was giving him. But being Andrew, he was too nice to push her back a step.

I was willing to do it for him. But it was Loke who intervened in the end, with a very convincing show of kindness, putting a hand on Heather's back. "You're shaking like a leaf right now. Why don't we sit down here and talk for a minute? Can I get you anything?"

And just like that, he had her out of Andrew's arms and sitting at one of the little picnic tables that Jessica had set up on the grass off the north end of the parking lot. She looked a little dazed, like she wasn't sure what had just happened. But she came to herself enough to snag onto Andrew's arm and make sure he sat on the bench next to her.

Loke and I sat down opposite her, and Loke handed her a packet of facial tissues. I couldn't quite tell where he had been carrying them. His pants were so tight that anything in his pockets would've totally shown. She took them with a murmur of thanks and dabbed gently at the corners of her eyes.

"You knew Dave Miller better than the rest of us, right?" I said. "You were in the same grade back in high school."

"That's right," she said. Then she looked up at Andrew. "You remembered me from high school?"

"Yeah, of course. You were a sophomore when I was a senior, but it's not like it was a very big school," he said.

"Dave Miller?" I prompted.

"Yes, I know Dave. Sorry, *knew* Dave," she said with a shaking sigh. "We were friends, I guess, but we never dated or anything like that. But that was all a long time ago."

"He came back into town to see you specifically?" I asked. Not adding, only thinking, that he had loved her deeply. And I really couldn't see why.

She half-shrugged. "That's what he says. Sorry, said. But that can't possibly be true. Can it? I mean, I'm pretty sure he was already here before I moved back in to my parents' place."

"I've never met Dave," I said, although the lump in my throat was calling me a liar if I meant I didn't know him. "But I've heard from multiple sources that's why he was here." Not that I thought it was true. But I wanted Heather's perspective before I laid my own cards down on the table. "Any particular reason why you doubt it? Was it a bad breakup? I mean, like a friendship breakup, since you said you two never dated."

"Not really," she said. "We didn't so much breakup as move away from each other and then just stopped calling each other a few months later. Zero drama. I went to college in Colorado but still spent my summers here, but he moved with his parents to Duluth to be closer to the hospital there. Both of his parents were pretty seriously ill. They were really old when they had him, and he's an only child. So instead of going to college, he moved with them to take care of them. But they both died within a week of each other just a few months ago. So that's why he's back in town. Nothing to do with me, really."

I closed my eyes for a moment, picturing my ink sketch. The gipt rune. My mind kept dodging away from the idea that this had ever meant a happy union between Dave and Heather. No, it was the other part of the meaning that Haraldr had warned me about.

Sacrifice. Dave had wanted a relationship with Heather, I knew that was true. And he probably would've followed her to college, gone to the same school no matter what their math program had looked like.

But instead, he had gone to Duluth. To be there to care for his parents in their last days. He had sacrificed all the possibilities for one kind of love to protect a more familial kind of love.

I respected that. A lot.

But clearly Heather didn't even grasp it.

I opened my eyes and looked at her again. She was fussing with the tissue in her hand, but her eyes were currently dry. And she had the look on her face of someone who is waiting for the current moment to be over so they can go on with other things. I could practically see her making a mental list of things to do as soon as she left my presence. I was barely holding her attention at all.

I resisted the urge to put a little commanding magic on my voice, to force her to respect what was happening here. It was what my mormor would do.

But it wasn't what I would do. Although in the moment I wished I could push the boundaries of appropriate uses of power just a little bit. But I wasn't built that way.

"Jessica said he'd been trying to see you," I said at last. "Like stalking you."

"It wasn't so bad as all that," Heather said dismissively.

"You seemed upset when he came to the mead hall last night," Loke said.

Confusion narrowed her super-blue eyes. "The mead hall?"

"That's what we locals call the bar in the meeting hall," Loke said smoothly.

"On account of my grandmother's mead," I added.

"Oh. Cute," she said and mustered up a ghost of a smile.

It was nice to know that the hall spells were working as intended, anyway. She remembered meeting us all and drinking mead together, but she had no memory of what the place had looked like, or of half of the people she had been dancing with beyond a vague sense of their faces. So my grandmother and I had gotten at least *that* much right.

"You were upset," Loke prompted.

"Well, Jessica was more upset than I was," Heather said almost sheepishly. "She's awfully protective. I mean, I appreciate it. It's nice having someone look out for you like that. But it was a little much sometimes." Then she fluttered her eyes up at Andrew again. "You heard she banned Dave from the café?"

"I did," he admitted.

"Yeah, that was excessive. I never asked her to do that," Heather said.

"Have the police spoken with you yet?" I asked.

She nodded. "Not that I could tell them anything. I don't know what happened. I wasn't even supposed to work today, not that I would've been here so early in the morning even if I were scheduled. They said he died before dawn. I definitely wasn't up that early. Not after last night."

"Do you have the keys to the café?" I asked.

"No. Jessica still does all the baking in the morning, so she's always here before me. And after me, too. I just help out during the rush times." She sniffled and dabbed her still-dry eyes again with the wad of tissues in her hand. Then she shot Andrew an imploring look. "You don't think she could've done this, do you?"

"No," Andrew said firmly.

"No, of course not," Heather agreed. "Not Jessica."

Loke nudged me with his elbow then pointed at the art bag I had set on the ground between my feet. I pulled out my sketchbook and pencils, turned to a blank page, then looked up to see Heather's face.

She was suddenly pale and very, very still. And she was looking down at my sketchbook as if I had just pulled out a gun and set it on the table between us. Aimed at her.

"Andrew, I have to go," she said, all in a rush.

"We were just going across the highway to grab some lunch and talk to Michelle. Are you sure you won't come with us?" Loke asked.

"Yeah, sorry," she mumbled. Then she looked up at Andrew again and gave him a much more heartfelt "sorry" before scrambling out of the picnic table and scurrying down the road towards Runde.

"What was that all about?" Andrew asked, turning in his seat to watch her jog away.

"She knew what you were about to do," Loke said to me. "And she didn't want you to do it. That's pretty interesting, isn't it?"

"Jessica must've told her… something," I said. I knew Jessica would never spill secrets that would lead anyone to Villmark, ever. But she must've said something about how I could know things about people just by drawing them.

I did a rough sketch from memory, but it was just a drawing. No magic senses were evoked. I put the book and pencil away.

"Shame," Loke said. He had been watching me draw, chin resting on his hand.

"I'll pin her down next time," I said. "She's definitely hiding something, isn't she?"

"Besides her natural hair and eye color, you mean?" Loke said drily.

I had the sudden urge to smack my own forehead. Colored

contacts. Of course. That was why her shade of blue was so heightened. Because it wasn't naturally occurring.

"What does she normally look like?" I asked Andrew.

"Just, you know," he said, but ended with a shrug.

"He doesn't remember her," Loke stage-whispered to me.

"It was a long time ago, and we never had any classes together," Andrew said defensively. "She's looked like she looks since she came to town. Or since I met her here again, anyway."

"She certainly seems to remember you," I said. I felt my cheeks heating even before I heard how jealous those words might sound. Especially when spoken in the tone I had just used.

"No, that's a new development, I promise you," Andrew said, his discomfort palpable. "She doesn't act this way when Jessica is around."

"You might want to nip that in the bud, yeah?" Loke suggested. Andrew mumbled something I didn't catch but that made Loke's smirk kick up a couple of notches. "Or," Loke went on as his grin spread even wider, "next time you can ask her nicely to sit for Ingrid to draw her. I have a feeling if you asked, she wouldn't say no."

"I'm not going to ask you to do that," I said, and Andrew gave me a relieved smile. "But let's go see Michelle and get something to eat. I'm starving."

CHAPTER FOURTEEN

IT WAS NEARLY two in the afternoon, and the restaurant was mostly empty. There was only a couple lingering over coffee and the remains of French fries on their plates at one of the booths, and a single truck driver at the counter scrolling through his phone as he dunked a grilled cheese sandwich into a mug of tomato soup. Michelle and Anna were standing together at the front register. They had been looking at something and talking in low voices, but stopped when we came in through the door.

"Have you learned anything?" I asked hopefully.

"Tons," Michelle said. "Not sure if it will be useful, though. Should we sit?"

"Sounds good," I said. Then I whispered to her mother while pointing discreetly at the truck driver. "Can I have what he's having?"

"Sure thing," she said. "What about the rest of you?"

"Same," Loke said, and after a moment's thought, Andrew nodded too.

"I'll bring it out in a jiffy," she said, and disappeared into the kitchen.

"Have you heard from Jessica yet?" Andrew asked as we slid into the same booth we had been sitting in before.

"Not yet. Sorry," Michelle said. "But I did run home to get this," she said, and set a battered yearbook on the table. She turned to a marked page. "This is Heather Peterson here."

I looked at the black-and-white photo. If Michelle hadn't pointed her out, I never would've guessed it was the same person as I'd just been talking to. It was difficult to tell just what color her hair and eyes were in the photo, but they definitely weren't light blonde and deep blue. "Wow, she looks different now," I said.

"That's kind of her thing," Michelle said, then turned to a different marked page. "This is Dave Miller."

I leaned forward to get a better look at the photo. I had never seen his face at the mead hall the night before, and when I had visualized him to sketch him, I had only seen the back of his head. And yet he looked exactly the way I thought he would look: the square head and broad shoulders of a football player combined with the nerdiest steel-framed glasses I had ever seen.

Andrew took the book from me when I was finished and examined the photo as well with a confused frown.

"What is it?" I asked.

"I remember him now," Andrew said, tapping the photo. "And her too, I think. Only I don't remember them together. Wasn't there another guy?" He looked at Michelle.

"It was high school. There were probably a bunch of other guys," she said.

"No, there was someone…" He trailed off as he turned the pages, scanning all the faces.

"What did you mean when you said it was kind of her thing?" I asked Michelle.

"Oh, Heather was always changing her look. Still does, actually. She didn't blow into town looking just like Jessica, I can tell you," she said.

"Heather looks like Jessica?" I asked. "I thought it was the other way around."

"Why would you think that?" Michelle asked.

"Well, I guess now that I know those are contacts she's wearing, it makes more sense..." I started to say, but I had to stop. It made no sense to me at all. "Wait, she is *trying* to look like Jessica? Why?"

"Who knows?" Michelle said with a shrug. "She just imprints on people and then copies them."

"That's creepy," Loke said.

"Tell me about it," Michelle said.

But something in her tone prompted me to ask, "She copied you?"

"That's right!" Andrew said, suddenly sitting up straighter. "I remember that. She worked here for like a month or something. That's where I saw her with that other guy."

"She worked here very briefly," Michelle agreed, then got up to help her mother carry the tray with all our soup and sandwiches on it. Andrew turned his attention back to the faces in the yearbook while Loke and I dove into our food with a little too much gusto.

But two in the afternoon is really late for breakfast, especially when you've been up since dawn.

"I had forgotten all about Heather working here until Mom said something about it. That's when I went home to get my yearbook. To jog my memory," Michelle said as she slid back into the booth. Her mother clicked her tongue as she leaned against the back of the seat behind Michelle.

"That poor girl was a little touched in the head," she said. "And that boy was always lurking around. I didn't like it."

"You mean Dave?" I asked.

"Yes, that's the one," she said. "He never caused any trouble, but he was always around when she was meant to be working."

"They were dating, right?" I said.

"No, he wasn't her boyfriend," she said.

"Wasn't he?" Michelle asked.

"That's what I've been telling you," Andrew said from behind the yearbook. "There was another guy."

"If you mean the hockey player, he was definitely not her boyfriend either," Anna said.

"Hockey player?" Michelle echoed while Andrew turned to an entirely different section of the yearbook.

"Oh, I know you remember him, dear," her mother said. "He used to come in here all the time with his friends from the team. They were hard to miss; they always wore their jerseys when they came in. Well, they weren't here *all* the time, actually. Only when you were working." She caught my eye and gave me a conspiratorial wink, then headed back to the front so the couple waiting at the register could pay their bill.

"Hockey player?" Michelle said again, but less vaguely this time. Like she was focusing in on something in her memory.

"Hockey player," Andrew said, and set the yearbook down in the middle of the table triumphantly. "This guy. Kristofer Meyer. He was a junior when we were seniors, but he was the star of the team even as a freshman. You *must* remember him."

"You know I worked too much to go to any games," Michelle said, but pitched her voice low so that her mother wouldn't overhear. But she took the book and examined the face Andrew pointed out in the team photo. "Oh, yeah. I remember him. He was always sweet. And a good tipper. But you know I didn't date in high school. I was—"

"Always working?" Loke finished for her with a mischievous gleam to his eye. "As opposed to now?"

"I take nights off," Michelle said, crossing her arms defensively. "Last night, for instance."

"Still no dates, though," Loke pointed out. She shot him a glare that, if it paled in comparison to Jessica's famed death glare, made me very glad indeed that I had never been on the receiving end of either of them.

"Is he still in town, do you think?" Andrew pondered.

"Oh, I'm sure not. He got a hockey scholarship to some east coast school, didn't he? Or maybe it was Chicago. Far away from here, I'm sure," Michelle said.

I pulled the yearbook over to look at the photo myself. I scanned all the faces, but all the northern European faces in hockey hair were blending together.

"It's this one," Michelle said, tapping one of the heads. I leaned closer.

Those eyes were very familiar. If you changed up the hair, cut off the back and sides but left a little of that wave in a tighter curl now on top...

"Oh, he's still in town," I said, not quite sure why I was grinning. But I was.

"How would you know?" Michelle asked suspiciously. Andrew was looking at me quizzically as well.

"I've seen him twice now," I said. "He was at the mead hall last night, just on the edge of the dance floor. And he was right here this morning, having breakfast at that very counter."

"Mom!" Michelle called, sounding almost alarmed. Her mother stopped bussing the table across the room and hurried over. "Mom, Ingrid says he was here this morning during the breakfast rush."

"Who, dear?" Anna asked.

"Kristofer Meyer," Michelle said, and took the yearbook out of my hands to shove it at her mother. "Was he here?" She tapped the picture aggressively.

"I think I'd remember that hair," Anna said. "Honestly, I mostly remember his jersey from when he'd come in before. What does he look like now?"

"He's still in good shape, like in that photo. But the hair is different. Shorter, but thicker curls on top?" I said, then pulled out my sketchbook to do a quick drawing.

"Oh, him. He's been in here a few times, actually. Sweet young man. Good tipper," Anna said.

"Why?" Michelle demanded of the room at large. "Why is he here? Heather works across the street!"

"Oh, he was never here to see Heather, dear," Anna said.

"Obviously," Loke put in.

"But you said you saw him and Heather together," Michelle said to Andrew.

Andrew held up his hands as if worried he was going to have to ward off some blows. "That's just what I remember. But my memory is all a muddle. Consider me an unreliable source."

"She was looking like you," I said suddenly. The words surprised even me, but I ran with the thought. "She changed her hair color to your hair color, and matched your ponytail. Working here, she already had your uniform, right?"

"It was only for a month, though," Michelle said. "It was creepy and invasive, but it was only for a month."

"So what happened?" I asked.

"Mom fired her," Michelle said, and Anna, once more standing over her shoulder, nodded.

"Yes, but what happened between her and Kristofer?" I pressed.

Michelle exchanged a look with Andrew, but at his shrug, she turned to look up at her mother.

"Sorry, dear. Once she was out of the restaurant, I never really thought about her again," Anna said.

"But she stopped trying to look like you," I said.

"Yeah. I mean, it took a while for the hair color to grow out. But she stopped putting it in a ponytail. And she didn't have the uniform anymore," Michelle said.

"So did she stop being you because she wasn't around you? Or because she got what she wanted? Presumably Kristofer?"

"This doesn't make any sense," Michelle said, slumping forward to put her hands over her face. "If he was coming here all the time to see me, how come *I* never knew anything about it?"

"You can be kind of oblivious," Loke said. I jammed him hard with my elbow.

"And now she's trying to look like Jessica," Michelle went on, her voice muffled by the hands still pressed to her face. "To get to Dave? That doesn't make any sense."

"No, Dave is a different category," I said. "I think he was always in her friend zone. I'm not seeing all the connections yet."

Which was putting it mildly. I was more and more sure I was missing an entire piece to this puzzle.

"But right now, I need to speak to Kristofer," I finished.

"Group text away," Andrew muttered as he started tapping at his phone.

Michelle lifted her face out of her hands to look at me. "You saw him at the mead hall last night?"

"Yeah, briefly," I said.

"And what was he doing?" she asked.

I shifted uncomfortably in my seat. "He was watching the dancing on the dance floor."

"But, like, me or Heather?" Michelle asked in the barest squeak of a voice.

"I'm sorry. I really don't know," I admitted.

"We'll find out for you," Loke said.

"Oh, we will, will we?" I turned to ask him.

"Well, *I* will," Loke said. "Just between you and me, your powers of observation are running at an appallingly low level these days. The things you're missing, it staggers the mind."

"All right, all right," I grumbled. "They were obviously contacts making her eyes so blue. I get it now. Give me a break. We were up all night. I'm running on fumes here."

Andrew looked up from his phone at that, his eyes darting from me to Loke then back again. I gave him a quick shake of my head. He thought it over, shrugged, then went back to his phone.

That was probably my own fault, for saying it made more sense to think I was a couple with Loke than I was with Roarr. Not that I had said that to *Andrew*. But things were getting needlessly complicated.

I longed for a little more of the gipt rune in my life. Two lines crossed. Simple.

But this murder case was shaping up to be a nightmare tangle of interlocking romantic triangles. I could never just pluck one out to examine it, because it dragged up all the others with it.

"He's been back in town for a few months now," Andrew said, reading from his phone. "Longer than Dave and Heather by quite a bit, if that matters."

"It might," I said.

"He's not always here, though. He's been working as a long-haul trucker, so he's gone days at a time," Andrew went on. "But I have an address for him. And it's one you already know."

"Really?" I said. I had no idea what he was referring to.

"Yep. Remember the apartment over his parents' barn where Garrett Nelsen was living? Well, Kristofer has been renting it out since coming back to town."

"That's not as weird as it sounds," Michelle said. "The rental opportunities around here are not what you'd call robust."

"Sure," I said. "But you're right. That is handy. We know right where to go. Shall we?"

"I'm still working, I'm afraid," Michelle said.

"If you hear from Jessica, text me," Andrew said as we all slid out of the booth and headed towards the door.

"The same goes for you if you hear from her first," Michelle said, and gave him one last hug.

Then the three of us were back out in the hot June afternoon, ready to burn off our lunch calories with a long walk over the bridge, down the bluffs and into the river valley where the farms of Runde lay.

CHAPTER FIFTEEN

Kristofer Meyer wasn't home, and Garrett Nelsen's mother had no idea when he'd be back in town. But, given that he had just left that morning to make his pick-up in Duluth to be delivered who knew where, it was probably going to be a few days before he got back.

And no, she wasn't going to let us see his apartment when he wasn't home. If the police came with a warrant, that was a different matter.

For the second time that day, I was tempted to magically oomph my voice. I didn't know which was more worrisome, my growing paranoia or this sudden thirst to flex my power.

Only, I probably should've listened to that paranoia sooner. Jessica wasn't in the kind of trouble I had been worried about, but she was definitely in some kind of trouble.

"Now what?" Loke asked after we were back on the north side of the highway bridge, right at the crossroads again.

"Not a clue," I said. "Short of drawing Heather, or breaking into the café to draw the space at the top of the stairs, I'm all tapped out."

"Well, I'm going to head back to my grandpa's service station for now," Andrew said. "The cell service is better there."

"Right," I said. "You'll let me know when they release Jessica?"

"Absolutely," he said. He gave me a little wave, then jogged across the broken pavement to the front door of the gas station.

"The police are still inside the café," Loke said. "Is there anything you can draw from here? I've seen you do remote work before."

"Yeah," I said, but I wasn't feeling it. "No, that's no good. I'm too tired and too distracted. It's not going to be worth the effort."

"Head back to the trailer and catch a nap?" Loke offered.

That was tempting.

But it also didn't feel like the right answer.

"No, let's try getting into the mead hall again," I said.

"You don't have to ask me twice," Loke said.

But when we reached the doors, they were still barred. There was a note from Keith expressing his confusion over the barred doors and a request to be called if he was needed for work that day.

"Maybe the back door?" I said. Loke shrugged. Neither of us was optimistic, and indeed it, too, was firmly locked.

Loke said nothing, but when I headed over to one of the tables on the far end of the patio, he followed behind me.

"You see spells, right?" I said.

"Not the way you do, I don't think," he said. "It's more like a different sense than sight, really. They kind of hum, but it's not really a sound. And sometimes there's an electric... something not quite a smell. It depends on the spell."

"The spells that maintain the mead hall are like a dense weaving, like a spiderweb but more deliberate," I said.

"That makes sense," Loke said with a sideways nod of his head. "Your mormor does love to knit. Your magic, I assume, is more like a drawing."

"What I've learned from my grandmother is like weaving. What I do myself is more like art," I said after a moment's thought.

"That's all very interesting, but how does it help us here?" he asked.

I took out my sketchbook and turned to a blank page. "The spells are easier to see on this side, the side closer to Villmark. But when I'm looking at the building, it's still all aluminum siding and steel fire doors. I'm going to try drawing to see what shows up."

"I know Thorbjorn helps you somehow, but I really don't know what I can do," he said. "Unless you wanted to pull from my power again like you did to jump back in time."

"I *definitely* don't want to do that again," I said. "I think I just want your help looking at the sketch when I'm done. You might see things that I don't. Or sense them," I amended, remembering his own words.

It took a couple of basic sketches to get into flow state, but the third time I turned a page and started again, I was no longer in control of what my pencil was doing on the paper. The next few minutes passed in the blink of an eye and then I was suddenly sitting back, sucking in a deep breath.

"Always unsettling when you do that," Loke mumbled, but I was smoothing the page with my hands, searching the image.

I had drawn a Viking long house, just as I saw the mead hall after sunset, particularly from the Villmark side.

I had also drawn the spells all around it. They extended up into the sky, something I had never seen them do in real life. They glowed white against the heavily darkened pencil background of the night sky, but they had contours like smoke or clouds did in Japanese woodblocks.

"Interesting," Loke said as he leaned in close next to me.

"What?" I asked, not sure what had caught his attention. He gently hovered a finger over the same plumes of smoke I was examining, careful not to touch and potentially smudge the paper.

"Don't you see it? Look at all the bind runes. And they're all different."

I picked up the sketchbook to hold it at a better angle to the sunlight dappling through the maple tree above us. I had to squint before I saw it, but Loke was right. I hadn't defined the puffs of magical power with mere lines. No, those lines were created from sequences of very tiny bind runes.

I knew what bind runes were, back from when I had used them in some of my Viking-inspired art. Back before I had even known my heritage as a volva. In fact, every phone has a bind rune icon built into it: the rune hagall for H and bjarkan for B that together had originally meant King Harald Bluetooth. Of course it meant something different now. Most people didn't know it was a bind rune at all.

In general, bind runes were ways of layering one rune on top of another to combine their linguistic meanings, like someone's initials becoming only a symbol.

Or to combine magical meanings, to work more powerful magic.

But I had never learned how to create magical bind runes. Not yet. That was knowledge that had to wait until I had a working knowledge of the individual runes first.

"Is this how I'm interpreting my grandmother's spells? In bind runes?" I wondered. "A few look like things I know, at least well enough to make a stab at their purpose. But I'm barely a third of the way through the futhark. I have so much left to learn."

"Isn't it a good sign, though?" Loke asked. "You understand enough that your mind wants to express what you can only sense in the form of bind runes. I think it means you're on the right path."

"It also means these spells are way more complicated than even I thought before," I said glumly. "How am I going to be any help at all?"

Loke stared off into the sky for a moment. There were clouds overhead, big puffy white ones that moved slowly by, unhurried by any wind or hint of an approaching storm. "Why does the magic go up so high?" he asked.

I looked in the same direction, but all I saw were clouds. "Does it?"

"You drew it going up and up forever," he said, still looking up into the sky.

"Maybe it doesn't mean anything," I suggested.

"Yeah, right," he said skeptically. "It means something."

"I wish I could see inside the building and be sure Mormor was all right," I said. But then I put my sketchbook away and got up from the table. "Come on. Let's check the cave to Villmark again."

Loke and I climbed the trail up to the cavern behind the waterfall, but the cave dead-ended with no sign of the opening that should be there. We even tried taking the smaller, narrower path that led down to the lower cavern behind the point where the waterfall ended, where the Villmarkers kept their boats hidden. But it was sealed off too.

"You want to try parting the water to get into the shipyard?" Loke asked.

"I haven't done that in ages," I said. But we went back the way we'd come until we were standing on the banks of the river in Runde, facing the waterfall head-on.

I took out my wand and repeated the magic my mormor had taught me the day we'd first gone out on Lake Superior in the longship with the other Villmarkers.

The waterfall parted in two like a curtain, far more easily than I had expected. I had grown so much in power and control over the last few months; it was easy to take that for granted.

But all that was visible behind it was rock. The entrance to the hidden lagoon was gone as if it had never been.

"Would it help to draw this, too?" Loke asked when I had let the waters fall back into place and put my wand away.

"Doubtful," I said, rubbing at my head tiredly. That nap was sounding better by the minute.

But it still didn't feel like the right thing to do.

"Let's go back to the café," I said.

"You want to try sneaking inside past the cops?" Loke asked, a little too eagerly.

"No, I was going to start with the parking lot. See if I could pull up and draw the scene when Jessica drove Dave away. It feels like a pivotal moment that I'm not getting a good bead on."

I started leading the way back up to the crossroads, but when we'd reached the far side of the mead hall, Loke caught my elbow and pulled me closer to my grandmother's trailer.

"No naps!" I said.

"No, but I'm thinking we can take a shortcut," he said. With his hand still firmly on my elbow, he opened the flimsy door to the trailer, then jumped up and through the doorway.

And out the front door of the café, sending us spilling and stumbling over the front walk and onto the gravel of the parking lot. Right between the two police cars.

"Are you crazy? Someone could've seen us!" I hissed at him, looking around to see if anyone had.

A truck blasted past us, but there was no other sign of humans about.

"Sorry. I guess I keep wanting to make sure I can still do it," Loke said sheepishly.

"Did you picture Villmark or here?" I asked him.

"Villmark first," he admitted. "Then here, when that didn't work out."

"Do you want me to try drawing your sister again?" I asked.

"No, let's focus on this case for now," he said.

We sat down at the same table where we'd questioned Heather before, only this time I was facing the parking lot and not the opposite side of the picnic table. Then I drew the scene before me. I tried pencils, then charcoals, and finally even ink, but nothing summoned any image besides the geographical features that were always there. I couldn't evoke the moment in time I was searching for.

"You should just pull from me again," Loke said with a sigh.

"Not if you're not okay with it," I said.

"I wouldn't have offered if I wasn't okay with it," he said, and held his hand out to me.

"Hold on," I said, and took up my pencil to draw a fast and loose sketch. Everything in the parking lot was there: the cars, the highway, the signpost. But I drew them all only on the edges of the paper, like a frame for a central image that simply wasn't there.

Only then did I take Loke's hand.

"The drawing is a doorway," I said.

"Like before," he said.

"No, not like before. This time, you're coming with me."

He opened his mouth to protest, but too late. I was already through the page, and Loke went through just behind me, his hand still in mine.

CHAPTER SIXTEEN

WHEN I HAD USED Loke's help to travel through time the month before, we had been standing beside the true ancestral fire of Vill-mark. That fire was a creation of my ancestress Torfa, who was likely the most powerful volva to have ever lived. Physically moving my body through time via a drawing and Loke's own brand of magic had only been possible because of the power emanating from those flames.

So where Loke and I found ourselves wasn't precisely in the café parking lot of an earlier June afternoon. No, where we were was a drawn simulation of that space. Like, literally. The world around us was all pencil strokes, if three-dimensional pencil strokes. I kicked at the gravel and it crunched under my foot, but in a muted sort of way. And I could feel the sun on my shoulders, but its warmth was greatly diminished.

"Neat trick," Loke said sardonically. When I looked over at him, I saw that he too was now nothing but a three-dimensional pencil sketch.

I looked down at my own hastily drawn hands. I hadn't spent much time drawing myself, ever. But I had drawn Loke many times. I hoped that was why he was so much better rendered in this world than I was.

"No, this is good," I said. "We don't have to worry about disrupting the time stream or anything."

"What does this tell us that your drawing didn't, though?" he asked.

Which was a good point. There was nothing going on around us except what I had put there with my pencil before we jumped in. What if this wasn't going to work?

But before I could say anything to Loke, the door to the café banged open. Or as much as it could bang in this penciled-in world where every sound was so muted. Then a sketch version of Dave Miller was marching out of the café, towards the two of us.

I grabbed Loke tighter and pulled him with me until we were both half-cowering behind the picnic table. Dave had a hand to his face as he walked, pushing up his glasses to press at the bridge of his nose, so it wasn't surprising that he didn't seem to notice us.

The door opened a second time, more quietly than the first, and a sketched Jessica emerged, jogging to catch up to Dave.

"We've discussed this, Dave," she said, and he stopped walking to turn and face her.

"I know. I'm sorry. I just... I need her help. I think she can help. Or I hope she can. I literally have no one else to ask," he said desperately.

"She doesn't even want to talk to you, Dave. I can guarantee she's not going to help you," Jessica said, crossing her arms and staring him down. Both she and Dave were proportioned correctly in this sketch world, but something in her body language was projecting her as being bigger than he was.

And he was scrunching up like Roarr did, making himself smaller.

"I don't know what she's told you, but I've never done anything to make her treat me this way," he said miserably.

"She's not given me any specifics. But I don't need them. If she says you're scaring her, that's all I need to know," Jessica said, still glaring for all she was worth.

"I don't mean to scare her," Dave said. Then he heaved a big sigh.

"You're right. I can't keep trying to talk to her if she's not going to listen. I'll go. You can tell her I won't bother her again."

"Go, like leaving town?" Jessica asked, her rigid body language suddenly softening.

"No, not yet," he said. "But I won't be coming back to the café. So you don't need to worry about me."

"The job market here is not great," Jessica said to him. "I don't know what's here for you to stick around for."

"No, but there's a million reasons not to go back to Duluth," he said with another sigh. He shoved his hands deep into the pockets of his jeans. "I need to make another plan. But until I do that, I might as well stay here as anywhere else."

"Look, if you're in some kind of trouble, I have friends who can help you out," she said.

"I thought you thought I was trouble. Like, a stalker, or whatever," he said.

"Honestly, I don't know, okay?" Jessica said, throwing up her hands. "I just know your presence upsets Heather. She's not faking that fear."

"Are you sure?" he asked. "Heather is… I don't know what Heather is. But she's not normal."

"She's been through something," Jessica said in a low murmur, although the only people around to overhear were Loke and me, and we kind of didn't exist from her perspective. "Like I said, I haven't pried, but she needs support right now and I'm trying to give her all I can."

"Why? You two were never close in high school or anything," Dave said.

"I'm doing it because she needs it, but also because I need to do something good right now. And never mind why," she said, a little edge back to her voice again.

"No, not my business," Dave readily agreed. "For what it's worth, I didn't come into town because I was chasing her or anything. I didn't even know she was here until I got here. And she's not the only one who's been through some stuff."

"Well, like I said, if you need help with anything, I can put you in touch with my friend Ingrid Torfa. She's good at helping people. You don't have to tell me what's going on, but you should tell her," Jessica said.

I could feel Loke looking at me now, but my eyes were still fixed on the two of them.

"Maybe I'll do that," Dave said. But it didn't sound like he meant it.

"Just please, stay away from the café, all right? If Heather changes her mind, I'll be the first to let you know. But for now, stop trying to see her. Okay?"

"Okay," he agreed with a solemn nod.

And then he turned and walked away.

Jessica stood alone in the parking lot for a minute, arms wrapped around herself like the gentle breeze was chilling her as it wafted through her loose hair.

Then she turned and walked back into the café.

I took Loke's hand and the two of us leapt back out of the drawing and sat gasping at the picnic table. I felt like I had been underwater holding my breath for far too long and black explosions were trying to dominate my vision.

But they cleared without me actually fainting.

"That was intense," Loke said. "I don't know if I'd want to do that again."

"Well, we did learn a bit, though, didn't we?" I said, looking down at the sketch before me. It was the same as it had been when I had jumped into it. No new details. I put the sketchbook away.

"What did we learn, exactly?" Loke asked, rubbing at his temples as if to massage a headache away.

"First of all, I know the sound in there was all weird, but nothing about that interaction matched the shouting that could be heard from across the street that we've been told about," I said.

"No, it was a remarkably friendly conversation for someone being kicked off someone else's property," Loke said. "Is that an effect of the spell, do you think? Maybe we saw a version of things that's not necessarily the true one."

"I don't know," I admitted. "But something else has been bugging me."

"What's that?" Loke asked.

"Last night in the mead hall, Jessica said she had something she wanted to talk to me about, but not there. She was going to talk to me today, actually. But she gave me no hint of what she wanted to talk about," I said.

"Yeah, I don't think that's at all related to this," Loke said with a hint of a smile.

"Why not? We just heard her telling Dave he should come talk to me," I said.

"I didn't get the sense she had any idea what was going on with Dave, only that he seemed preoccupied with something she thought you could help with," Loke said. "In which case, she would've told you something more like she had someone she wanted you to talk to. Not that she had something to tell you."

"Maybe she wanted to talk to me about Heather," I said.

"Or maybe it was about something else all together," Loke said.

"I don't know where else I could go to draw more about Dave," I said.

"His parents' house? New owners now, but if all his high school angst is tied up there…" Loke finished with a shrug.

"No, despite what everyone keeps saying, I just don't think this is about high school. Or, at least, not *entirely* about high school." I said.

"You want to know more about what his life was like in Duluth," Loke guessed with scary accuracy. "How's your car doing?"

"Honestly, not a clue," I admitted. "It's not been driven all winter. I'm pretty sure the odds are against it even starting now. But even if it did, I can't leave town now."

"No, I'd prefer if you didn't," Loke agreed. "I would feel compelled to go with you, and I *really* don't want to leave town now."

"Do you want me to draw your sister again?" I offered.

"No, I'm sure she's fine," he said, almost convincingly. "But you were having another thought. About Duluth?"

"Well, it's not like I don't have friends there," I said. As he well knew. He had been with me in Duluth the day I had run in to my old coworker Jesús Rodríguez from the diner back in St. Paul. Out of the blue, just sitting on a bench.

Like I had summoned him there by magic.

And he had brought us to his sister Tlalli, who I later found out was something like the Aztec version of a volva.

"True," Loke said. "And they've helped us solve a murder before. I'm sure they'll step up again."

"Dave was going to school part-time, right? It's just possible he was at the same school as Tlalli," I said. I pulled out my phone but saw no texts from Andrew, Jessica or Michelle.

No news wasn't exactly good news. But at least it wasn't bad news.

I pulled up my group text with Tlalli María Rodríguez and her brother, Ichtaca Jesús. She went by Tlalli these days, but he still preferred his Spanish name to his Aztec one.

I had known Jesús throughout my art school days and back into my later high school days. But not from school; we had worked together in the same diner. We had been the first two to always volunteer for overtime, so we had worked a lot of shifts together. We'd probably spent more time with each other than either of us had spent with our families.

Then I had come to Runde to live with my grandmother, and he had moved to Duluth to stay with his sister while she worked her way through college.

And yeah, like Loke had pointed out, he and his sister had helped me solve a murder that had started in Duluth but ended on Lake Superior off the shores of Runde.

But as I texted them both everything I knew and everything I was hoping they could find out for me about Dave Miller, I couldn't help thinking that both of them were so much more than amateur investigators. Because Tlalli was also a wielder of magic who came from a hidden city in Mexico, one so hidden that she had yet to re-find it. And Jesús too had a sort of destiny beyond working in diners.

I wasn't getting the sense that magic had any part to play in what had happened to Dave Miller. But it was nice to know that if it had, the Rodríguez siblings were more than capable of dealing with it.

When I finished what was probably too many texts to send all at once, I put my phone away and looked at Loke.

"Now what?" he asked.

"Now we're back to waiting," I said with a sigh. "But let's go wait back at the restaurant. I need more coffee."

"We could break into the café here and brew some of Jessica's far superior beans," Loke suggested.

Which was tempting. It really was far better coffee.

But.

"Michelle is at the restaurant, and likely Andrew as well," I said.

"Fine. Have it your way," Loke said as he pushed up from the picnic table. "But if I get cranky from the cheap stuff, that's all on you."

"Well, I'll be cranky too, so how am I going to notice?" I said.

Then we crossed the street to the restaurant, whose coffee we both knew was perfectly fine. But honestly, we were both cranky already.

Neither of us were waiting people. And yet, what other choice did we have?

CHAPTER SEVENTEEN

IT WAS STILL TOO EARLY in the afternoon for the dinner rush at the restaurant, so it wasn't too surprising when Michelle was waiting to meet us at the door.

"Any news?" she and I asked each other at the same time.

"You first," she said.

"I'm still working on some leads, but nothing concrete yet," I said. I glanced at my phone, but neither of the Rodríguez siblings had responded yet. Well, it had only been five minutes. He was probably working. She was either working or in a class or doing homework. I could give them *ten* minutes to respond, surely.

"Where's Andrew?" Loke asked, looking around the empty restaurant.

"He went to the police station to wait for Jessica to be released," Michelle said. "Not that anyone contacted us about that. It was more of an… aspirational decision."

"Well, it looks like it worked out," Loke said as he craned his neck to look out the windows that faced the highway. "That's him now, and Jessica is with him."

"Oh, thank goodness!" Michelle said, her whole body going limp with relief.

We stepped back from the door enough for the two of them to get inside. But Michelle instantly lunged forward to give Jessica a hug so fierce it looked almost painful.

"No charges?" I asked.

"Not yet," Andrew said, but his tone was grim.

"Let me guess, they said not to leave town," I said.

"It's all right," Jessica said to me, but just looking at her, I could see things were very far from all right. I had never seen her looking so terrible, pale and exhausted with wide, frightened eyes. She looked like a rabbit that was starting to realize there was no escape from its tormentors after hours of trying to flee.

"She doesn't have an alibi, and her prints are almost certainly on the murder weapon," Andrew said.

"When are they placing the time of death?" I asked.

"Sometime between the point when Heather and I left the mead hall last night—or rather very early this morning—and 6 a.m., which is when they discovered the body in the café," Jessica said.

"Why don't we sit down?" Loke suggested. Jessica nodded but still clung tightly to Michelle. Michelle guided her over to what was rapidly becoming *our* corner booth and got her settled before immediately tearing off to fetch coffee. Jessica summoned enough energy to slide over and make room for Andrew to sit beside her, but then lapsed back into a barely awake sort of catatonia.

"The police found the body," I said as I sat down across from Jessica.

"They said they were answering an anonymous call. Someone saw lights inside the café, like there was a break-in in progress or something." Her voice was barely there, her tone dead as if giving us the same rote answers she'd already given at the station many, many times already.

"Anonymous, in this town?" Loke said skeptically. "Who would see? The restaurant wasn't open yet, and neither was the service station. Someone passing on the highway? At highway speed?"

"It seems suspicious, right?" Andrew said to me.

"It certainly does to me," I said.

"But not to the police," Jessica said dully. Andrew gave her a look of concern that echoed my own.

"Jessica, I know you've had a very long day already, but I could really use your help. I have so many questions that I'm afraid you're the only one who can answer," I said.

"I know. Ask away," she said, and made an attempt at stirring herself up to a more receptive listening posture.

"Who moved back to town first, Heather or Dave?" I asked.

"Oh," she said, as if surprised that was the first question. "I saw Heather first. She had just moved back into her old bedroom in her parents' house the night before she came to see me in the café about a job. She didn't mention Dave then, but I'm pretty sure he was already here." She chewed at her lip a little too aggressively, and I reached across the table to give her hand a reassuring squeeze.

"It's okay. Whatever you remember," I said.

"No, I'm thinking," she said. "I can't prove it. I didn't see him until at least a week after Heather started working with me. But I'm pretty sure he was already here. But I can't say why. It's just a feeling."

"I put a lot of stock in instincts and feelings, you know," I said. "And not just my own."

"I know," she said. But she wasn't cheered by my words as much as I had hoped.

"Were you at the café at all between the time you left the mead hall and when you were picked up by the police in the morning?" I asked. "I don't know, doing a little inventory in the middle of the night or anything at all?"

"No," she said. "I wasn't doing fresh baking that morning, on account of knowing it was going to be a late night at the mead hall, right?"

"So, when you left the mead hall, you went straight home?"

"Pretty much," she said. "Heather and I left at the same time, so we walked together. Heather's house is a street over from mine, so I walked a little bit out of my way, but not much. I didn't come up to the highway or anything like that."

"Did the police find any evidence of a break-in?" Andrew asked.

"Not that they told me," Jessica said. "I supposed if there had been, they would've said something?" She directed that question at me.

"I don't know," I said. "Is it possible someone stole your keys or something?"

"No, I had them with me when I left my house to walk to the café in the morning," she said.

"Heather was with you after the mead hall until you were practically home," Loke said. "How is it they don't consider that an alibi?"

"Because the murder happened after," I said.

"Also, my mother is visiting her sister in Superior, Wisconsin, so she's not home," Jessica said. "I was alone in the house. Allegedly," she added darkly.

"Hey, you know we all believe you," Andrew said to her gently.

"I know," she said, not quite looking up at him.

"How hard did you come down on Dave when you banned him from the café?" I asked.

She blinked. "I don't think I was hard on him at all. Did someone say I was?"

"Shouting was mentioned," I said vaguely.

"No, I don't think I was shouting at him," she said. "I was firm. I had to be firm. But I wasn't… unhinged."

"I didn't think so," I quickly told her. "You wanted him to come see me, right?"

"Right," Jessica said, but her brow was furrowing in confusion.

"Magic," Loke put in. "We sort of saw the whole conversation, Ingy and I."

"Right," Jessica said again, this time with more understanding. "I'm not as good as you are with reading people, but I was getting a vibe off of him. I mean, he was scaring Heather. Making *that* stop was my first priority. I wanted Heather to feel safe, you know? But after that, I wanted him to feel safe, too. And I had a feeling like he didn't."

"He didn't feel safe?" I asked.

"He never said anything to that effect, but yeah."

Michelle finally reappeared with a tray of coffee cups and two full carafes. We took a minute to disperse them amongst ourselves, then I scooched over on the bench to let Michelle sit beside me. Jessica took her cup with shaking hands, but the coffee seemed to revive her a little before my very eyes. There was an alertness in her demeanor that hadn't been there before.

"My feeling about that, and about him being here before Heather, I think they're related," she said. "He says he was moving back here now that both of his parents have passed, but he wasn't looking for work or anything. He was just staying out of sight. I only met him the few times when he tried to talk to Heather. I never saw him around town otherwise."

"He was hiding from something?" I asked.

"Again, he didn't say so," Jessica said.

"But your gut said he was," I guessed, and she nodded as she took another long sip of her coffee.

"Where's Heather now? Do we know?" Andrew asked.

"Presumably at her parents' house," I said.

"Were you going to talk to her again? Or try drawing her?" Andrew asked.

"I still might, but I want to know more about something else first," I said, then glanced at my phone resting beside my coffee cup. Still no texts. "I'm waiting to hear back, actually."

"From who?" Michelle asked.

"Tlalli and Jesús," I said. "They live in Duluth, where Dave was before he came here. I don't know what they'll be able to find out. It might be nothing, or nothing useful. But I agree with Jessica. Dave was here for a reason that wasn't Heather. She just got tied up with him later. Something else drove him here."

"I can't imagine what that could be," Jessica said. "He's a pretty withdrawn guy on the best of days. And he had his hands full since leaving Runde, taking care of his parents. How did he even have any time to get into any trouble?"

"Maybe trouble found him," Loke guessed.

"Like I said, I hope to know more soon," I said. "Then, depending on what I hear, I'll try talking to Heather again."

"Did you want me there for that?" Andrew asked. He was blushing furiously, and I could just tell he was really hoping I'd say no.

But I couldn't. "Probably," I said with a sympathetic wince. "Loke's not wrong. She *is* more likely to let me draw her and ask her more questions if you ask her to. And I'm sorry, if it's important and we have no other leads, I might have to change my mind about asking you to. I don't think she'll listen to anyone else."

"Really?" Jessica asked, giving Andrew a probing look.

"It's a thing," he mumbled, looking down at his own hands. "A new thing."

"Not a welcome new thing," Loke added helpfully.

Jessica was still looking at Andrew questioningly, but he was studiously refusing to look back over at her.

"Jessica," I said, and she shifted her gaze back to me. "Last night at the mead hall, you said you wanted to talk to me later. Like, today later."

"Oh, that," she said with an airy laugh. She shot nervous little glances at everyone else around the table. "That was nothing. I mean, nothing important. It was nothing to do with all *this*."

But her eyes on mine were desperately imploring, and I knew whatever she still wanted to talk to me about, she didn't want to do it around any of the others.

"You're sure?" I asked. "It wasn't about Heather or anything?"

"No, it isn't," she insisted. "We can catch up once all this mess is dealt with. It really wasn't as important as all that."

I doubted that very much. But I knew she wasn't going to say anything more with the others all gathered close around her. So I would have to let it drop for the time being.

"What now?" Loke asked and then yawned hugely. Which had me yawning too, hard enough to make my jaw pop.

"You two look exhausted," Jessica said. Which was saying something, coming from her.

"I woke them up early," Andrew said.

"We were also up late," I said. And immediately regretted it as Jessica looked at me with concern.

"Because of the mead hall? Did something go wrong?" she asked, her hands twisting together.

"Everything is fine," I assured her. A total lie. But she looked relieved, so I guess it was a lie I had told convincingly enough.

"Nothing for you to worry about," Loke added. "But I think Ingy and I should check up on some things before it gets dark, yeah?"

"Yeah," I agreed. "But if something comes up, come find me, okay?"

"Certainly," Andrew said.

"I should go, too," Jessica said.

People were starting to come into the restaurant, the tables around us slowly filling with customers. Anna on her own was staying on top of it so far, but I could see her looking towards Michelle to find a good moment to interrupt.

"Your mother is still out?" Andrew asked Jessica, that concern back in his voice.

"Yeah, but I'll be okay," Jessica said.

"I'll come over as soon as my shift is up," Michelle said even as she got to her feet. "Three hours tops. I don't want you alone in that house tonight."

"Thanks, Michelle," Jessica said with a grateful smile.

"I'll stay with her until you get there," Andrew said to Michelle.

"Get some food into her," Michelle ordered. Then she was crossing the restaurant at a rapid clip, her professional smile already in place to greet the pair of customers who had just come in the door.

"Do you want me to come too?" I asked Jessica.

"No, you and Loke sound like you have something important to tend to," she said. "Something important but also secret. I get it."

"Villmark business, really," Loke said.

"I get it," Jessica said again.

"I know you do," I said, and gave her a quick hug. "But I'm always just a phone call away. If you need me, I'll be there as fast as I can."

"I know you will," she said. Then she looked over at Andrew. He seemed lost in thought, staring unseeingly at the empty coffee cup in front of him. Then, as if he could feel all our eyes on him, he shook himself out of it and slid out of the booth in a hurry. He turned as if to help Jessica out, but I stepped up closer to him first to speak close to his ear.

"I don't think she's in danger, but I can't be sure," I whispered to him. "Maybe hang around even after Michelle gets there? If you can?"

"I will," he promised.

"Thank you," I said. He nodded, looking more embarrassed even than when we'd all been talking about his effect on Heather.

"Someone hates being seen as a white knight," I mumbled to Loke as we headed out the door.

"Sure. That's what that was," Loke said. Before I could ask what that meant, though, he was talking again. "We're going to check on Mormor, right?"

"Right," I said. "Hopefully she's solved everything while we've been chasing our tails, trying to solve our own thing."

"Well, I wouldn't get my hopes up too much," Loke said. I gave him a questioning look, and he said, "Every time we step through a door, I've been trying to get back to Villmark. None of my attempts have worked yet. Including through the two sets of doors we just passed through leaving the restaurant."

So it wasn't entirely surprising to find the spells over the mead hall locked up just as tightly as they'd been when I'd seen them last.

And so were the doors to the Runde meeting hall.

We were zero for two, solving our problems that day.

Loke followed me back to the mobile home without a word of protest. We must have been thinking the same thing.

Without a good night's sleep, we stood little chance of doing anything productive. But getting a good night's sleep with all the worries on our minds was going to be a trick in itself.

Luckily, the minute I collapsed onto the battered couch in my grandmother's sitting area, it was a trick that I pulled off on the first try.

CHAPTER EIGHTEEN

For the second morning in a row, I woke up totally disoriented on the couch of my grandmother's temporary sitting room.

With someone pounding loudly on that flimsy door.

The sun was just past the trees, coming in through the front window at the perfect angle to completely blind me the minute I opened my eyes. I heard motion in the room, Loke stumbling towards the door. I moved out of the sun and blinked a few times until the spots started fading.

"Hey," I heard Loke say after opening the door.

"Hey, yourself. Is Ingrid up?" I heard Michelle ask.

"I'm up," I said, rubbing at the back of my neck as I crossed the small room to the door. I had a pronounced crick in my neck from sleeping slouched back on a couch rather than in a proper bed for two nights in a row. I also had a sizable knotted snarl of hair that went way beyond bedhead. This was going to call for the creamiest of rinses.

Or a pair of scissors.

"You weren't answering your texts, so I came down to tell you that Kristofer Meyer is back in town already," she said when I appeared in the doorway beside Loke.

I took a moment to recall all the conversations from the day before. "The hockey player and truck driver?" I said.

"That's him," she said. "You said you wanted to talk to him."

"I *did* say that," I admitted. But that had been before I had settled my mind on the murder not really involving anything that happened in high school.

Well, there was always the chance that my hunch was wrong.

Also, with no leads to followup, the only other thing to do was wait. And I hated waiting.

"Did you want to come with us?" I asked. Loke had taken half a step back, presumably to give me more room in the tiny doorway. But I could also feel his fingers touching the back of my hair. Examining that knot.

"Oh, no! That would be really awkward," she said, flushing.

"Loke and I knocking on his door has to be at least a little more awkward, as we've never even met him," I said.

"Well, given the questions we're going to be asking him, being strangers is probably better than being friends he's lost touch with," Loke said. He was still gently fussing with my hair. As if he could untangle that hopeless mess.

"We were never really friends," Michelle said. "And anyway, I have to work today."

"We'll give him your regards," Loke said gallantly.

"But I want to check on Mormor first," I said, mostly to Loke, but Michelle nodded her understanding.

"Kristofer just came in at dawn. My mother served him breakfast. He's probably sleeping now, but that means he's not going anywhere. So you'll know just where to find him," she said. Then she glanced at the screen of the phone in her hand. "But I really have to get to work. Any news from Duluth?"

"I'm not sure," I said, looking around for my own phone. It wasn't in my hand or my pocket.

"Well, let me know when you know something, okay?" she said. "Jessica isn't opening the café today since it's still technically a crime scene, but Andrew promised to stay with her. Just in case."

"That's good to know, thanks," I said. "I'll stop in at some point today for sure, whether I have news or not."

"Sounds good," Michelle said, then waved goodbye to the two of us and started jogging back towards the path that led up the steep bluff side to the crossroad.

"Hold still," Loke said when I tried to turn around to look for my phone.

"You're an agent of chaos. The odds of you bringing order to my hair have to be pretty close to zero," I told him.

"And yet," he said, and lifted his hands away from my hair.

I touched the back of my head. It still needed a good brushing, and a wash wouldn't be a bad idea if I only had the time. But at least the fierce tangle was gone.

"Thanks," I said, impressed despite myself.

"Your phone is charging in the kitchen," Loke told me. "In case you forgot, that's where you put it."

"The end of last night is a bit of a blur," I admitted as I headed towards the kitchen.

"Which is pretty funny, considering I think it was like eight o'clock when you crashed," he said.

"You were up later?" I asked as I moved past my phone to start some coffee first.

"A bit," he said drily.

"You tried to get back to Villmark," I guessed.

"Tried and failed," he said. "This is two days now."

"We're going to solve this today for sure. I promise you," I said.

"We should get back inside the café," he said. "The police must be gone by now. If you drew the scene of the original fight, we might learn something useful."

"I agree," I said. "But maybe we should talk to Kristofer first?"

"Well, check your phone first," he said. "It's been buzzing all morning. I'll take over with the coffee."

I grabbed my phone and sat down at the kitchen table, scrolling past dozens of texts from Tlalli and Jesús both.

It was a lot of information to scroll through.

I tried putting a call through since it would be faster to catch up talking than reading and sending more texts, but as was all too often the case down in the Runde river valley, I couldn't get more than a warbling, unreliable connection that wouldn't hold long enough to be answered on the other end.

So I scrolled back through the texts and started at the beginning. There were a few texts from after eight the night before, mostly just the two of them clarifying what they were about to dig into. Luckily, they hadn't waited around for me to respond, since I had been dead to the world for nearly twelve hours.

"Dave Miller was a student at the same college that Tlalli is attending," I told Loke as I read through the texts. "Only part-time, and only since January, though."

"She had classes with him?" Loke asked as he took clean mugs out of the cabinet.

"No, she works in the administration office part-time as a work/study thing and logged into one of the computers with a password that was super-easy to guess, apparently," I said. "Dave was already enrolled for fall semester, full-time class load. So he had made plans to stay at *some* point."

"Something definitely happened in Duluth, then," Loke said as he brought me a cup of coffee.

"Something sudden, or he would've withdrawn from the college," I agreed. "Only what? And was he still hoping to go back? Jessica said he was never looking for work around here, which doesn't sound like he intended to stay. How much cash could he have left to live on?"

"What else does she say?" Loke asked as he sat down across from me with a mug of his own.

"Not much," I admitted. "She's handing a list of every classmate from the two classes Dave was taking from January to May to Jesús, and he's going to track all of them down if he can."

"Good luck in the middle of summer," Loke said drily.

"Yeah, a lot of them would've gone home for the break. But he's got their phone numbers too. Hopefully, he learns something. But Dave lived off campus, so no roommate is listed in the school system." I sighed as I drummed my fingertips on the tabletop. "This might end up being another dead end."

"Give it a day, anyway," Loke said.

We both downed the coffee faster than was strictly advisable, as hot as it was, then headed out into another sunny, warm June morning towards the meeting hall.

It was still locked.

"Do we give this another day as well?" Loke asked.

"No," I said. "Let's go talk to Kristofer, then hit the café, and then come back here. If my grandmother is still locked inside, I'm going to start seeing what magic *I* can wield to bring this door down."

"Seriously?" Loke asked.

"You don't think I can do it?" I asked.

"No, I wouldn't say that," he said. Then that familiar grin was back on his face. "I'm saying I'm going to really love seeing you try. I'd even be willing to let you pull everything you need out of me. Do you want to do it now?"

I closed my eyes for a moment and let my magical senses expand around me. But I sensed no danger, no trouble, nothing to raise alarm.

I *could* sense my grandmother still within the walls of the mead hall. Magic was dancing around her, at her bidding.

"No, not yet," I said to Loke when I opened my eyes. "She's still working on it. And as annoying as it is that she's giving us no updates, breaking down the door is still a little premature."

"In that case, shall we take a shortcut?" he asked, sweeping his arms back towards the flimsy door to my grandmother's mobile home.

Considering that walking to the Nelsen farm would involve going up the bluffs to the highway, then taking the bridge across to the other side and down more bluffs to the other side of the valley, how could I refuse?

Loke gripped the doorknob then flung the door open with a flourish that sent it crashing against the side of the house again. I had felt his momentary hesitation as he had visualized where he wanted us to go. It had been a little long for picking one destination. So he was still trying Villmark again first. Always trying Villmark first.

Not that I could blame him.

We emerged from a back door to the Nelsens' barn, out of sight from the house itself. Which suited me fine; the fewer people I had to talk to, the better.

We climbed up another narrow outdoor staircase to a second level apartment, but this was newer and far sturdier than the one that had led up to Dave Miller's apartment. And the apartment above was more spacious as well, I remembered from when I had been out here before looking for clues to Garret's murder.

I knocked briskly and heard someone moving around inside almost at once. I entertained a brief hope that we had caught him unwinding before bed. But when he opened the door, he was wearing only pajama bottoms and was rubbing at his hair tiredly. He focused his eyes on me for a long moment before deciding he definitely didn't know who I was.

"Can I help you?" he asked. He didn't sound half as irritable as I would if our roles were reversed.

"We're sorry to wake you," I said. He just nodded, waiting for me to go on. "I'm Ingrid Torfa, and this is my friend Luke. We're hoping to ask you a few questions about Dave Miller and Heather Peterson."

"Dave and Heather? Whatever for?" he asked, genuinely perplexed.

"You know them, right?" I said.

"I did in high school," he said. "What's this all about?"

"So you haven't heard the news?" I said. He shrugged. "Dave was murdered yesterday."

"Murdered?" Kristofer repeated, and reached out to clutch the doorframe as if to hold himself steady.

"Have you seen him recently? Since he came back to town?" I asked.

"I didn't even know he was *in* town," he said. "I don't think I've talked to him since graduation. No, I *definitely* haven't. Or Heather either. Just how is she mixed up in all this?"

"She's also back in town," I said.

"Okay," he said, still sounding confused. Then he looked up at me, his brown eyes intense. "How am *I* mixed up in all this? Because I came back home too?"

"You all knew each other in high school," I said with a shrug.

"Well, that's hardly amazing. Everyone in this town and the nearest three towns besides went to the same high school," he said. "It's a close-knit community."

"Some people are knit closer than others," Loke said.

"Well, sure," Kristofer said with a frustrated sigh. "Look, Dave was a friend in high school. Not a close friend, but he tutored me in math. I don't think I would've graduated without his help, and no graduation would've meant no hockey scholarship. I owe him a lot, and I'm sorry to hear he's dead. That means I'll never get the chance to repay him, on top of just the tragedy of it all."

"And Heather?" I prompted.

"Heather Peterson," he said, chewing at his lip as he tried to summon up any memories. "I think she was dating my little brother at one point? I don't really remember her particularly well. Just that Dave would mention her from time to time. He was always looking out for her."

"And warning people away from her," I said on impulse.

He frowned at me for a moment, then something lit up in his eyes. "Oh, yeah, right. No, she *didn't* date my brother. She was trying to get *me* to ask her out. I remember now because Dave was the one who told me I definitely didn't want to get mixed up in that."

"Why?" I asked.

"He had reasons, but I really didn't listen to them, to be honest," he said. "I had no intention of dating her in the first place, so it wasn't like I needed a warning to stay away."

"Why didn't you want to date her?" I asked.

"I wasn't dating anybody in high school," he said. "I was very focused on hockey. I really wanted that scholarship. It was my one way out of this town, you know?"

"And yet, here you are," I had to say.

"I was a star player for my college team until I tore up my knee my junior year," he said without any particular bad feeling. Like it was just a thing that had happened, not an entire life's dream derailed. "I recovered well enough to play again, but not at the level I had been at."

"Focused on hockey," Loke said from behind me. "That was all?"

"Me not dating Heather had nothing to do with Heather, all right? It was entirely a 'me' thing. That's all I can tell you," Kristofer said.

"Because we have it on good authority that you used to hang out at the restaurant with your teammates on a very regular basis," Loke went on.

"What does that have to do with anything?" Kristofer asked, confused again.

It said a lot about him that even recently woken up after driving his truck for who knew how long, his confusion wasn't fading into annoyance or anger.

"Heather worked in the restaurant," I told him. "For a time."

"I don't remember her there at all," he said with a shake of his head. "Sorry."

"She looked a lot like Michelle at that point," I said.

His cheeks flushed a little at the mention of that name, but he just shrugged again. "I don't remember anyone looking like Michelle. Except for Michelle."

"But you remember Michelle," Loke said as if scoring a major point.

Kristofer's flush deepened a little. "Well, yeah. She's still there. Who can forget her?"

"So neither Heather nor Dave tried to get in contact with you after coming back to town?" I asked.

"How long have they been here?" he asked.

"Just a few weeks," I said.

"No, I haven't heard from either one of them," he said. "I've been here for five months myself, but I've been keeping it low-key. They might not have known I was here to look up."

I looked at Loke, but he just shrugged.

"Well, thanks for your time. And, again, sorry to have woken you up," I said.

"No problem," he said. But he shut the door on us before we could come up with any other questions.

"You're right," Loke said as we walked back down the stairs. "High school is definitely a red herring in all this."

"Maybe," I said. "I mean, I'm not getting a vibe from anyone that they're lying about anything."

"For all we know, this is just some random serial killer thing," Loke said. "It happens."

"Yeah, but not in Jessica's basement, it doesn't," I said. "And not with a perp who looks like it could be Jessica or Heather, or at the very least, a not particularly bulky woman."

"To the café, then?" Loke said, reaching for the same barn door we had used to travel here.

"To the café," I said.

There was that same long hesitation as he again tried to reach Vill-mark first, and then he opened the door to show the darkened interior of the empty café.

And I followed him inside.

CHAPTER NINETEEN

WE WEREN'T in the basement this time. Instead, we stepped out of the restroom at the back of the café, just behind the little kitchen. I went past the kitchen to the main area of the café, emerging between two bookshelves.

To my right, all the computers in her internet café area were shut down. It wasn't just that the monitors were off; someone had shut down every single computer. I had been here after-hours before, but I had never been here when the hum of PC fans wasn't a constant presence. Its absence made the sound of passing cars and trucks on the highway outside all the louder.

The eating area was tidy, chairs pushed in under the gleamingly clean tables and the napkin dispensers all full and ready for customers that wouldn't be coming today.

There were still a few scones and cookies in the display counter, looking quite dry but not yet molding.

"Do you think the police will be back?" Loke asked as we stood looking into the case. "We could clean up a little if no one was going to notice."

"I'm sure they'll let Jessica in tomorrow to clean up," I said.

"They've already gotten all the evidence they're going to. Don't you think?"

Loke just shrugged.

I finally turned to look at the door that led to the top of the stairs down to the basement. I had only rarely seen Jessica go through there, usually to bring up clean laundry or a box of supplies from the storage area. I had never seen it left standing open before. But it was open now, and it wasn't hard to tell why Jessica always made sure that door was locked.

The stairs started just inside the door, and they were nothing but bare wood, no treads or anything to keep feet from slipping on them. And they were narrow and steep. It really wouldn't be hard for someone to trip and fall all the way down them to the dirt floor below.

And it would be easier still to push someone from the hallway.

"Why would anyone stab him with such a tiny knife first?" I asked as Loke and I stood at the top of the stairs. I found the switch and turned on the light, and we could see all the evidence markers still arranged on the edges of the stairs and across the floor below. "A simple push would've killed him just as easily. And honestly, how would anyone know it wasn't an accident? It's not like that knife could've even hurt him much."

"I know this guy wasn't particularly athletic, but he was big all the same. Perhaps without the momentary distraction of the knife injury, his murderer would not have succeeded in pushing him at all. It's a narrow doorway. He could've caught the frame," Loke said.

"It just feels irrational, you know?" I said.

"A crime of passion?"

"Maybe?" I said. "But I don't necessarily think this was spontaneous. Maybe it was planned ahead by someone who had no idea what they were doing. I mean, whoever did it seems to have lured him here after-hours. Was it to kill him or just to talk to him?"

"Well, there's a way to find out," Loke said, raising his eyebrows at me significantly.

"Right," I said, and walked to the nearest table to set my art bag down on one chair and myself on another.

"I'm going to quietly poke around the kitchen," Loke said. "Not that I think I'll find anything."

"Okay," I said as I dug my sketchbook and pencils out of my bag. "You've said you don't like watching me do this."

"I'll help interpret when you're done. Just give me a holler," he said. Then he let himself behind the counter and disappeared into the back.

I half-suspected he was less looking for clues than just trying the door from the kitchen to the hallway that led to the restroom in the hopes of somehow reaching Villmark, but it's not like it mattered. The police had been here for hours. I doubted very much they had missed anything.

Except for the things only I could see.

I pulled another chair around so I could rest my feet on its seat, then arranged my sketchbook on my raised knees. This time, I deliberately let the gipt rune flow through me for a few minutes before trying an actual magical drawing.

I really had to make the time to meditate on it soon. It was like it was trying to burst out of the inner recesses of my mind, no longer willing to be ignored.

But even as I filled a page with nothing but Xs, I couldn't help musing on the meaning of it. Two people together, giving and receiving, both sacrificing to the thing they created together that was bigger than both of them.

Dave had tried to protect Heather from the world, and the world from Heather. But Heather never reciprocated. That was too one-sided a relationship to really be related to gipt.

Heather had pursued Kristofer in a way that sounded to me like she was only trying to keep him and Michelle apart. Which was ironic since they were never actually together. That was even less related to gipt.

Heather's sudden interest in Andrew I didn't understand at all. So I quickly pushed that from my mind.

But my pencil kept drawing not so much an X as the two halves not quite joining in the middle. Like reversed brackets, > <. That wasn't the rune, and it definitely wasn't a bind rune.

But it was something.

I had a sudden hum in my brain, a strange new sensation for me. This wasn't how insights usually announced themselves to my conscious self.

And yet I was absolutely sure that somewhere in all this mess was a pair that wasn't joined. A pair that was sacrificing their togetherness for something else, something greater, maybe?

I chewed at the end of my pencil. That could be Dave, giving up on pursuing Heather for the sake of his parents. Only Heather had never sacrificed anything. So that didn't make sense.

But the feeling was so strong. It was like it filled the café. That being-apart-for-someone-else's-sake feeling was centered in this place. And I hadn't felt it in the basement.

But then again, the murder hadn't happened in the basement. It had happened up here, and then rolled down the stairs.

I turned the page, an automatic gesture because I was already in my fugue state. Then I lost all awareness as my pencil worked all over the page, filling in detail after detail too fast for my eyes to follow.

When I was done, I was looking at a series of three images. In the larger, central image, the woman I had drawn at the top of the stairs before—whether she was Jessica or Heather or someone else entirely, I still didn't know—was standing behind the counter with her back to me. She was up on tiptoe, doing something to the coffeemakers. Putting something inside them, maybe? It was hard to tell from behind.

In the final image, I recognized Dave's back between me and the counter. The woman had turned around, but his shoulder was blocking my view of her face.

But not of the little knife in her hand. Dave had his hands out away from his sides, palms just starting to turn up. Imploring her to be calm, maybe?

Most curious was the first of the three images, the first and the smallest. It was two people leaning against the back bumper of a pickup truck under a dim streetlight, apparently talking. I could see my grandmother's mobile home in the background dimly and guessed this was the mead hall parking lot the night before the murder.

The man's face was hard to make out, but the streetlight was gleaming off his glasses. That and the build of his body led me to presume this was Dave again. But who was he talking to?

"Who's that, then?" Loke asked, so suddenly it made me jump. He had sneaked out of the kitchen to stand right behind me without me even noticing. Now he leaned forward to examine the same small drawing I was looking at.

"I don't know. She's not familiar," I said.

"Definitely not Jessica," he said. "I don't think it's Heather either."

"No, I agree," I said. Then a sudden memory struck me, and I sucked in a breath.

"What?" Loke asked.

"The night at the mead hall," I said. "Wait, you were with me when I saw her!"

"Her?" he asked, pointing at the sketchbook skeptically.

"I think so," I said. "Jessica and Andrew had already gone back inside, Heather with them. Then you and I walked up to the doors, and this woman came out. She looked kind of like them, but not exactly. I remember thinking I was crazy assuming Jessica was trying to deliberately look like Heather, that it was probably just a coincidence because here was this third woman with almost the same hair and almost the same clothes."

"You thought *Jessica* was trying to look like *Heather*?" Loke said.

"Never mind that now," I grumbled. I tapped the first drawing. "Dave was at the mead hall, but he didn't go inside. But apparently he didn't leave either, just lingered in the parking lot. Was he waiting to try talking to Heather again?"

"Jessica seemed very confident that he wasn't going to attempt that again," Loke said.

"And I tend to agree with her," I said. "So Dave came for his own reasons, but when he saw Heather, he quickly made himself scarce for her sake. But why hang out in the parking lot?"

"Maybe this other woman was who he was looking for the whole time," Loke said.

"But who *is* she?" I asked.

"Well, more importantly, what was she doing inside the café?" he said.

Then we both looked at the coffeemakers.

"The police were all over this place for hours and hours," Loke said, but I was already taking my wand out of my bag. I brought it with me behind the counter and opened the tops of the coffeemakers. They were filled with ground beans nestled inside the filters, just waiting for someone to push the button to turn them on.

I stirred around the grounds with my fingertip, but the smell that rose up was perfectly ordinary.

"The pumps weren't working," Loke said suddenly.

"What do you mean?" I asked.

"Jessica has pumps that bring the water directly from the filtration system by the sink in the kitchen. Only they were clogged. She had a work order for a plumber to come take a look at them posted on her board in the back," he said.

I got on my tiptoes to look further inside the coffeemakers. "There's water in here already."

"Someone filled them by hand," Loke said. "Like in that picture you drew."

"So this woman broke in to be helpful?" I said doubtfully.

Loke said nothing, but I sensed a shrug happening behind my back. I found a step stool and pulled it over so I could stand over the two coffeemakers. Then I waved my wand before my eyes.

I wasn't sure exactly what I was looking for, but when the water glowed an evil green, I was pretty sure I had found it.

"Do you think the police tested these water reservoirs for poisons?" I asked.

"If they had, they'd be emptier," Loke said. "How sure are you that they're poisoned?"

"Pretty sure," I said as I jumped down from the step stool.

"You could tell them to look," Loke said with the hint of a grin. "I'm sure they'd be willing to let the whole violating a crime scene thing go for good intel like that."

"Right," I scoffed.

Then the phone in my pocket vibrated. I pulled it out to see texts from both Tlalli and Jesús. They kept coming, first from one then the other, overlapping floods of information.

But Tlalli had included a photo in one of her texts, and the minute my eyes scanned over it, I was glad I had already gotten down from the step stool. Even standing on the ground, I had to grip the counter for support.

"What is it?" Loke asked.

I showed him the photograph on my phone. "Kind of looks like the woman from the sketches, doesn't it?" I said.

"Almost like Jessica, and almost like Heather," he agreed. "Who is she?"

I peered at Tlalli's text. "Melissa Scott, a nursing student at the same school that Tlalli and Dave attend."

"I think you've found your suspect," Loke said.

"Well, they did, anyway," I said, trying to scan through the rest of the texts. There were a lot. And they kept coming. I heaved a tired sigh. "This would be so much easier if I could just go to Duluth and talk to the both of them face to face."

"So why don't you?" Loke asked conversationally.

"Because even if I had a working car, it would take like an hour and a half to get there. With the time I'd spend talking to them, I'd be away for four or five hours. I can't do that right now," I said.

Like he needed me to point that out. He was more anxious to get back to Villmark than I was.

But he was grinning at me again.

"What?" I asked, too tired to try not to sound annoyed.

"Ingy, I've been to their apartment before," he said. "I know just what doorway to move through. We can be there in less than ten seconds."

Now I was grinning too. "You're handy to have around," I told him.

"I know," he said. Then he held out an arm for me to take.

We bent back down the hallway to the restroom door, then left Runde behind entirely, emerging through a very different bathroom door into a tiny Duluth apartment.

Where a very startled Jesús sat gaping at us from his dining table, his phone in one hand and a forkful of eggs frozen halfway to his mouth in the other.

CHAPTER TWENTY

JESÚS HADN'T CHANGED a bit in the seven months since I had seen him last. His long dark hair was still pulled back into a ponytail at the nape of his neck, so thick it always made me jealous. He was dressed in jeans and a neat button-up shirt, but something in the leisurely way he was eating his eggs at one in the afternoon told me he was coming off a morning shift, not getting ready for an afternoon one.

He set his fork of eggs back down on his plate, then got from up his table to pull me into a tight hug. After so many months among the towering men and women of Villmark, being hugged by someone whose head barely cleared the shoulder of my completely average height body was a little strange.

But short as he was, the arms squeezing me tight had a wiry strength I knew I was only feeling a fraction of.

"Hey, Jesús," I said, hugging him back. "Sorry to drop in unannounced."

"I'm not sure if you had announced what you were about to do that I would've even believed it," he said, finally letting me go. "Neat trick. My sister has learned a ton of stuff since we saw you last, but nothing remotely like that."

"In all fairness, it wasn't me," I admitted. "It was Loke."

Jesús looked over at Loke, who merely shrugged. And eyed the eggs hungrily.

"Can I get you guys something to eat?" Jesús asked, not missing a beat.

"No, we're fine. You just got off work, I can tell," I said.

"True, but scrambling eggs for two people is hardly what I call work," he said, despite my words already heading for the little kitchenette. "I have bell peppers and onions already chopped in the fridge, and the cast iron is still warm. Just give me three minutes."

"We are here rather urgently—" I started to say.

But Loke interrupted with, "We can spare three minutes, surely."

"You really can," Jesús said from the kitchen. "My sister is on her way home now, but she's still about five minutes away. You might as well eat while you're waiting."

There was no arguing with either of them, apparently. And I was hungry anyway. By the time Tlalli turned up six minutes later, the three of us were chowing down on scrambled eggs with onions and peppers and lots of hot sauce.

"Ingrid! You're here!" Tlalli said as she came in the door, a backpack over one shoulder and her arms full of file folders and a stack of mail. She dumped it all on a chair by the door before giving me a hug of hello.

Tlalli had the same short but strong stature as her brother, and the same thick, dark hair. But hers was in a long braid that hung down her back to her waist, tied off with a sparkling bit of red ribbon.

"They just came out of the bathroom," Jesús told her around a mouthful of egg. "Some kind of bathroom magic."

"Bathroom magic?" Tlalli repeated.

"Doorways, actually," Loke said.

"Well, whichever, I'm glad you're here," she said as she turned to dig one of the file folders out from the bottom of the stack of mail. "It's going to be easier to hand this to you than to text you photos of all of it."

"You found something out?" I asked as she handed me the folder.

"I found a lot out," she said smugly, then went into the kitchenette to retrieve the plate of eggs her brother had left for her in the warming drawer. Then she joined us at the little table. We were all overlapping elbows now, so I pushed my chair back after a few more bites so that I could open the folder and peruse its contents.

"I got that from the administrative office," Tlalli said as I looked at the now-familiar photo of Melissa Scott in the corner of a page filled with her personal information. Name, social security number, home address. The works.

"They just let you take this?" I asked.

"No," she admitted. "I was taking photos of the computer screen, because I didn't want to try sending you anything directly from that computer. It can be tracked, if anyone bothered to look. Which I doubt they would, and I was using someone else's password. But in the end, it seemed simpler to break into the file cabinets and get the paper file for you."

"And then text it all to me?" I asked as I turned past copies of Melissa's school application forms and previous transcripts.

"It's possible I had a niggling feeling like I'd be seeing you," she said with a mysterious smile.

"Your brother said your magical studies have been going well," I said. "I don't know how you find time for it on top of school and your work/study. I barely manage, and it's all I'm doing."

"My sister is a quick learner," Jesús said, and Tlalli blushed.

"I'm sure Ingrid is being modest," she said to him.

"So the mentor my grandmother recommended to you has been working out?" I asked. I hadn't been sure at the time how that would work. My grandmother and I were both Norse volvas, although I did more rune work than she did. But Tlalli's magic was Aztec, and yet her mentor was an Irish immigrant who followed a Celtic path.

"It's been great!" Tlalli assured me, and the enthusiasm radiating off of her felt entirely genuine. "She has access to a fairy barrow. Time stands still in there, or nearly so. It makes it easier to find the time for my magical studies."

"And I'm sure it has absolutely no cost at all," Jesús said mildly. "That kind of magic never really has any side effects."

I gave them both a confused look, but Tlalli just shot her brother an angry glare. "I know what I'm doing," she said to both of us.

"So, Melissa Scott," Loke said, drawing my attention back to the folder open on my lap.

"Right, have you seen her lately?" I asked.

"I went by her apartment this morning, but she wasn't there," Tlalli said.

"Work or school, I'm guessing?" I said, but Tlalli was already shaking her head.

"No, she's been gone for days," she said. "Her neighbor came out while I was knocking on the door to tell me so."

"One of *those* neighbors," Jesús said, rolling his eyes.

"Apparently her mailbox is overflowing, although how that affects her neighbor, I have no idea," Tlalli said.

"Did the neighbor have any idea when she left or where she went?" I asked.

"Something like three or four days ago, but she didn't know where," Tlalli said.

"I'm guessing Runde," Loke said.

"She was a nursing student?" I asked, and Tlalli nodded.

"Not in any of my classes. She's in her first year," she said.

"Would you say she'd have any knowledge of poisons at all?" I asked.

Tlalli set her fork down and looked at me sharply, as if to be sure I wasn't joking. "Lots of things are poisonous," she said at last. "Is there any one in particular you think she might have been messing with?"

"I don't actually know," I admitted. "I saw a green glow when I looked at it with my magical sight, but I don't know what that means."

"Depends on the green," Tlalli said, chewing at her lip. Then she got up and went into her bedroom. I could tell it was hers from the artwork on the outside of it. When I had been here before, it had been decorated with colorful skulls for the Day of the Dead. Now it featured a sun and moon with wise faces painted in fiesta colors.

She came back out with a small tablet and opened up an art program. She used her fingertip as a brush to make a swirl of color, then opened up the color options to tinker with the settings. When she was done, she showed me a blotch of venomous green.

"Was this it?" she asked.

"A little brighter," I said, reaching for the tablet. She handed it to me, and I adjusted the hue, saturation and brightness until I was confident what was on the screen was as close as I could get to what I remembered seeing. Then I handed the tablet back to her.

"Right," she said, and sat back in her chair. Her eyes drifted half-closed, and her brother beside her stopped tapping at his phone as if to lend her silence. Loke and I sat quietly as well, watching as Tlalli's eyelids fluttered and her lips moved in silent syllables.

Then her eyes flew open again, and she sucked in a deep breath. "Ricin," she said. "Or some sort of derivative or extract from ricin."

"Not the more traditional arsenic?" Jesús asked half-jokingly.

Tlalli shot him an annoyed look. "Arsenic would be lavender," she said.

"Right. Of course," he said. He caught Loke's eye and gave him a conspiratorial wink.

"So if we were to get inside Melissa's apartment, we'd be looking for, what, castor oil?" I asked.

"No, that's no good," Tlalli said. "Ricin isn't oil soluble, so there's very little remaining after the production process for castor oil."

"But if she condensed it down and concentrated it somehow?" I asked, waving my hands around vaguely.

"No, that's not it. What we'd be looking for is the beans them-selves," she said. But I could tell she was still thinking from the way she was tugging at her lip. "They aren't terribly dangerous in whole bean form because of the seed coat, but if she ground them up..."

She trailed off, but Loke filled the gap with, "And mixed them with coffee grounds?"

"They weren't in the grounds. They were in the water," I said.

"It's very rare to die from it these days anyway," Tlalli said. "Anyone with symptoms gets medical treatment and they recover. Unless it's given by injection, but you said in the water, so..."

"What if she just wanted to make a bunch of people sick?" Loke said. "Ruin a café's reputation. Destroy a business."

"Oh, it would totally do that," Tlalli agreed. "But so would easier things to acquire. Like eye drops, for instance."

"Why would this Melissa person even care about destroying Jessica's business, anyway?" I asked. "Assuming she was even in Runde, she would've been chasing Dave, right? So why go after Jessica? Jessica barely knew Dave."

"Maybe she thought it was Heather's café," Loke said. He tapped the corner of his eye, enough to remind me how much Heather and Jessica looked alike. If Melissa, who knew nobody, had seen either of them from a distance, she could easily mistake one for the other.

"How did she know Dave?" I asked.

"Ugh," Tlalli said, pulling a face as if the topic were just that unsavory. "Well, apparently they had an intro class together. Just a zero credit prep thing for students with gaps in their academic careers to ease the transition. The class was only for a couple of weeks before the start of the semester, basically over the winter break. But it left a very strong impression on the other students in that class. Not the class itself, of course, but the way Melissa immediately glommed on to Dave."

"Those were the words they used," Jesús told us. "Glommed on."

"It paints a picture," Loke said. "So Dave didn't reciprocate her affections?"

"Everyone says no," Jesús said with a shrug. "They never had another class together, so I'm sure Dave thought the problem would sort itself out."

"But she wouldn't let him go," Tlalli said, and pointed at the folder still resting on my lap. "She was actually given two warnings about her disruptive behavior. She would've been expelled, I'm sure, if Dave had ever been the one reporting her for harassment. But it was teachers whose classes she interrupted when she tried to talk to Dave."

"She interrupted classes?" I said, pressing a hand to my forehead. "To talk to a guy who didn't want to talk to her?"

"We should get her and Heather together," Loke mused. "They sound like they could be besties."

I dropped my hand to look at him. "What it sounds like is that Dave wanted Heather's help because he hoped maybe she'd have some insight into Melissa's behavior. Maybe even know how to stop it."

"Yeah, I've only had Intro to Psychology, but I'm pretty sure that was never going to work," Tlalli said drily.

"Melissa hasn't been here as if this morning, then?" I asked.

"Her neighbor hadn't seen her, and she hadn't picked up her mail," Tlalli said.

"Is she still in Runde, then?" Loke asked.

"I know a few location spells that might come in handy," Tlalli offered.

"I have a few things I can try as well," I said. Although I felt a pang in my heart. Most of the searching magic things I had done in the past had involved my cat, Mjolner. And he was apparently still trapped in Villmark.

"We should go back with you all the same," Tlalli said, and her brother gave her a look of surprise. "What? You don't work tonight. It's fine."

"I'm not arguing," he said. "Especially if we don't have to take the van. We can travel through bathroom magic."

"Again, it's the doorways," Loke said. Although I was pretty sure Jesús had remembered that just fine.

"If you're sure?" I said. "I mean, extra hands are always welcome, but Loke and I can probably handle this from here."

"Well, it's not just that, though, is it?" Tlalli said, giving me a significant look. One which I didn't understand at all.

Which apparently was clear from the look on my face.

"You don't even know what I'm talking about, do you? I was afraid of that. Come on," she said, and gestured for me to follow her out the apartment door. I signaled for Loke to wait for me, then followed Tlalli out into the hall.

But we didn't go down to the ground level. Instead, we went up two more flights to the roof. The heavy fire door was meant to be locked at all times, but gave with a loud click at Tlalli's gentle touch. Then we were out on a tarred, flat roof. There were no signs that anyone else from the apartment building ever came up here. No tables or lawn chairs or even empty cans anywhere in sight.

To the east was a pretty decent view of Lake Superior. Beyond the rooftops of the college buildings, anyway. But Tlalli walked all the way to the northern-most edge of the building. There was nothing to see here but treetops around the roofs of suburban homes. I could hear the highway, but it was out of sight beyond the last line of trees.

"Do you want to explain that?" Tlalli asked. She held her hand palm up and pointed it northward.

"Explain what?" I asked. There were wildfires currently burning in Canada, and the sky to the north was a haze of diffuse smoke that drifted out over the lake, obscuring my view of the water's far horizon.

But then I realized my first instinct, to look to the lake for signs of danger, was wrong. She was pointing towards Runde itself.

Or rather, the pillar of magical energy that jutted up into that smoky haze.

"It's been there for two nights now," she said, even as I gaped at it wordlessly. "And it's getting brighter by the hour. Yesterday, I couldn't see it in the daylight. But it's visible today. Any plans to bring that back down? I mean, aren't you supposed to be a hidden pocket universe? What's with the Biblical-level flare?"

"It's the mead hall," I said when I could finally manage to squeak out intelligible sounds. "The magic in the mead hall has gone all wonky."

"Well, then," Tlalli said, folding her arms. "Still think you and Loke can handle this fine without me?"

I looked at that column of magical light. There was no way my grandmother knew that was happening. Because if she did,she'd be stopping it.

And if she couldn't do it alone, she'd have called me in to help by now.

"No, for that, I definitely need all the help I can get," I said.

"Then let's stop wasting time and get going," she said, and headed back towards the door.

"If Melissa isn't here, she might be back in Runde. Only I don't know why. She might be planning to hurt more people than just Dave," I said.

"We'll stop her," Tlalli said grimly as she pulled the heavy door open again. "But those spells of your grandmother's have to be under control before nightfall. I don't even want to *think* about what kind of attention you'll be drawing once it gets dark again."

I didn't want to think about it either. Whatever my ancestress Torfa had been fleeing when she had brought her entire village here to the north shore of Lake Superior, it had been back in Norway.

And I had a feeling whatever she had been running from was still hunting for the people of Villmark. And didn't need eyes to sense power like what was shooting up into the sky.

And the curvature of the globe wasn't going to be enough to hide us either.

This had to be fixed ASAP, or all of Villmark would be in danger.

CHAPTER TWENTY-ONE

After a quick discussion with Loke and Jesús, we all agreed that getting the mead hall back under control had to be our first priority.

So it was a bit of an unpleasant surprise to find myself back in Jessica's café after walking through the bathroom door of their tiny Duluth apartment.

Worse than that, I was alone. I didn't even know that was possible, to move through doorways without Loke. I had been right behind him when I had stepped into the doorway. But now there was no sign of him or the siblings.

Then I heard something, not so much a crash as a rattle, but someone was definitely inside the café with me.

And my instincts were screaming it wasn't any of my friends.

Although it was still possible that it might be Jessica or Andrew or maybe even Michelle. But even as I told myself that, I couldn't bring myself to call out a hello.

Instead, I took out my wand, then set my art bag quietly down on the floor against the wall.

In that moment, I really missed my cat. I always felt safer confronting danger with Mjolner at my side.

But I was alone. So I pulled my shoulders back, lifted my chin, and crept towards the front of the café. The sound had been coming from the kitchen, but the door that opened up onto the hallway was closed, and I couldn't be sure to not be seen if I tried opening it.

So I took the long way, through the café dining area and up to the counter. As I drew closer, I could see someone moving around in the kitchen. At first glance, I might've taken it to be Jessica, if the last few days hadn't taught me to be too paranoid about Jessica lookalikes. Her back was to me, so all I saw was the blonde hair hanging loosely around the shoulders.

I recognized the shirt, a loose-fitting flannel shirt of purple, pink and sapphire blue that I had always admired. It was definitely Jessica's shirt.

But why was she wearing a shirt so heavy it could practically function as a jacket in the middle of summer?

I lowered my wand until it was out of sight behind the counter, then said, "Melissa?"

I couldn't tell what she was doing exactly. She froze her motions at the sound of my voice.

But she didn't turn around.

"Melissa Scott," I said, not a question this time. "Dave is dead. What more mischief could you possibly have to do here?"

"I don't know what you're talking about," she said, still keeping her back to me. Whatever she was doing at the prep table, she carried on with it as if I weren't there at all.

"You murdered Dave Miller," I said. "Right here inside this building. You stabbed him with one of Jessica's knives, then pushed him down the stairs. Because he rejected you, I'm guessing. More than that, he ran away from you. That made you pretty angry, didn't it?"

Melissa heaved a dramatic sigh and once again stopped whatever she was doing. Then she finally turned to face me.

The knife she had in her hand this time was not for scraping the seeds out of a vanilla bean. It didn't belong inside the café at all. It would probably even be overkill inside a butcher shop.

"That's not Jessica's knife," I said. I was a little incredulous at my own words. Was I trying for jokes now? I suppose it came from spending way too much time in Loke's company.

But it felt important to keep her talking. To buy for time.

When I didn't step out of Loke's doorway in my grandmother's trailer home, I was sure Duluth would be the first place he would go to look for me. But this, being the last door we had stepped through before that one, would be second.

Or so I hoped.

Because, as crazy as she was, I wasn't sure Melissa was unhinged enough for everyone to ignore her if she saw me doing magic before she was arrested. The police would probably discount anything she said that sounded fantastical, but I didn't want to rely on that.

That beacon of magical light blasting into the sky was making strict secrecy all the more important at the moment.

I tucked the wand into the back of my pants, then raised both my hands up to where she could see them.

"You don't need that knife," I said as I took a step back.

"I'm supposed to just let you go, and you'll never say a word to anyone about seeing me here? Please!" she scoffed.

"What happened to Dave could still be considered manslaughter, not murder. An accident in the heat of the moment. But killing me too? They'll never buy two accidents," I said.

"I don't know. Those stairs are a pretty obvious hazard," she said with a casual shrug.

"Yeah, I'm not sure they're quite up to code," I agreed.

Again with the jokes.

Melissa narrowed her eyes at me, like she wasn't sure why I was joking either.

"You poisoned the coffee," I said, deadly serious again.

"I did," she said smugly.

"Why?" I asked.

"Despite what you may think, I didn't come here to *kill* Dave," she said. She sounded exasperated, like she'd already had to explain this to me too many times before. "He ran here, sure, but he wasn't running *away* from me. He was running *to* her."

"To Heather?" I asked.

She gave me a puzzled look. "Who's Heather?"

"Dave's kind of girlfriend from high school?" I said, confused myself. "She came back to town right after he did."

"No, it was this Jessica chick he was always trying to talk to," she said. She gestured with that wicked knife as she spoke, and I involuntarily flinched a little as a random beam of sunlight caught the blade in a flash.

"Jessica was protecting Heather," I said. "She thought Dave was stalking her."

"She thought *Dave* was..." But she broke off with a harsh laugh. "Oh, that's rich."

"She had a sense that he wasn't," I said. "But she was still protecting Heather's sense of safety, even if she was never actually in danger."

"She sounds like a head case," Melissa said.

"No, she's just kind," I said. I still had my hands up where she could see them, but I pointed towards the coffeemakers. "You had no reason to try to poison her customers and destroy her business. She wasn't standing between you and Dave."

"No, she was kind of on my side, wasn't she?" Melissa mused. "She was standing between Dave and the actual girl he was running to instead of me." She glanced over at the coffeemakers and smirked. "Ironic."

"What are you doing here this time? Making sure Jessica gets framed for your crime? Because she doesn't deserve that," I said.

She actually blushed, as if she were capable of feeling embarrassment. "I was just being sure. I came here to do two things: to destroy her and to bring Dave back home with me."

"But Dave is gone," I said.

"That really was an accident," she said. "He wouldn't listen to me. He was trying to stop me. That knife in his back was just to get his attention. It was never going to do permanent damage. I'm not sure why he thought the basement was the better escape route away from me, but then again, I'm not sure what he thought he was going to accomplish coming to this rat hole of a town in the first place. So."

"You never considered you stood a better chance of getting away with it if you just left town right away?" I asked.

"Well, I came here to accomplish two tasks, like I said. Just because I failed at getting Dave home didn't mean I had to bail on my first mission," she said with a shrug.

"Only Dave wasn't running to Jessica. Or to Heather, for that matter. He really was running from you. I guess you couldn't bail on your first mission without admitting that to yourself."

She sneered, but didn't respond.

I looked past her, trying to catch a glimpse of what I had interrupted her doing. All I could make out were the canisters of flour and sugar that were always arranged along that prep table. Only every single one of them was standing with their tops off at that moment.

"Poisoning the baked goods," I guessed. "Ricin again?"

"Oh, nicely spotted. But no, for this I thought arsenic was the better call," she said with another casual shrug. "Tastes like almonds, you know. It would be nice in scones, I figured."

"But now you have to get me out of the way first," I guessed.

"Actually, I need you for something before I can kill you," she said.

"I'm not helping you poison people," I said.

"Like I need your help with that," she scoffed. "No, all I need from you is everything you know about this Heather person. Her last name, where she lives, that sort of thing. And don't bother lying. I'm very good at finding out what I need to know, so it won't do you any good to try hiding things from me."

In that moment, I heard something, like someone taking a sudden sharp intake of breath. But it was coming from the restroom at the end of the hallway, and with the door closed between the hallway and the kitchen, I didn't think Melissa had even heard it.

I carefully didn't react.

"As much as I'd like to see you try, I don't think you're going to get the chance," I said as I lowered my hands.

"What makes you say that?" she asked, pointing the knife at me. The sun glinted off the metal again, but this time I didn't flinch. And before I could answer, the door behind her exploded open and Loke charged through. He brought his fist down in a chop to her outstretched wrist, and the knife clattered to the floor. I heard it skitter over the tiles and desperately hoped it had managed to slide away somewhere inaccessible.

Not that it mattered in the end. Melissa sucked in a breath of frustrated pain from Loke's blow, but side-stepped his attempt to grapple her, pulling a pistol out from the back of her waistband in the same smooth movement.

How many times had she practiced that? It was like watching something out of an action film, well-rehearsed and flawlessly executed.

"Back up," she said to Loke as she trained the gun on him. She took a few steps away from him, well out of his reach, alternating between aiming the gun at him and at me. But her motions were too randomly timed for me to risk trying to charge her.

I really didn't want to know what getting shot would feel like.

I took another few steps back, and Loke was now back out of the kitchen and into the hallway. His hands were up, but his eyes were scanning everywhere for any kind of opening. If the knife were still in sight, his gaze gave no hint of it.

But to my right, I could see the door at the top of the basement stairs was standing open. It was the only nonmagical weapon at my disposal. And it would be a little tricky to wield.

Maybe a little too tricky.

I had no other options. I reached for my wand.

Then there was an explosion of noise behind me, and I was showered in bits of glass as one of the large rocks that marked out parking spaces on the gravel parking lot outside sailed through the front window.

I heard the sharp retort of the gun going off, too loud in too small a space. My ears were ringing as I dropped to the ground, heedless of the glass that pricked at my palms.

"Loke!" I yelled, my voice muffled in my own ears. I wasn't sure if I couldn't hear an answer because of the damage to my hearing, or because Loke wasn't capable of making an answer at all.

Then someone blew past me, boots crunching over the glass as they ran towards the café counter.

I knew those boots. It was Kristofer.

Even through my damaged ears, I could hear Melissa cursing angrily. Then the gun went off again, and the muffled tones from before became a constant high-pitched ringing.

I looked up in time to see Kristofer tackling Melissa. So he played a little football as well as hockey.

The gun fell from her grasp, but again I suspected she had some sort of fight training. Because try as he might, he couldn't get a strong enough hold on her to properly grapple and restrain her.

The two of them wrestled in and out of attempted locks. Then she ducked under his arm and gave him some sort of short blow to the back of his neck. This seemed to stun him for half a second, but not long enough for her to get completely away. He spun and tackled her again.

And they both disappeared from sight, down that cursed flight of stairs.

I heard voices, faintly under the ringing in my ears, and then Michelle was running past me towards the top of the stairs. Then Andrew and Jessica were there too, rushing to join her in that doorway looking down.

A hand closed over mine and I looked up to see Loke. I was still on my hands and knees, and he had crawled his way over the glass to get to me. But aside from superficial cuts on our hands and a complete inability to speak to each other, we both looked okay.

"Kristofer?" I said, probably too loudly, but I couldn't quite hear my own voice.

I could see Michelle say something before she charged down the stairs to the basement. But it didn't matter that I couldn't hear her. The look of sudden relief on Jessica's face told me enough.

Then Andrew was at my side, helping me and then Loke to our feet. Jessica joined us as we all stepped back out through the broken window into the surprisingly gorgeous June afternoon.

"What happened?" I asked, trying not to shout.

"Kristofer is okay," Andrew said. "That Melissa woman took the brunt of the fall. She's hurt and not moving too much, but she'll survive."

"In prison," Jessica said bitterly.

"What happened *before* that?" I asked. The ringing was fading, but not fast enough.

"I called everyone," Loke said. "Although what I told them was to stay put and keep a watch out for danger. Not to go *looking* for it."

"You said Ingrid was in danger," Andrew said.

"I said she *might* be, and that I had it under control," Loke said.

"It doesn't matter. It's all over now," I said. Although I couldn't help but feel a little glow of happiness. It was nice to have friends who would throw themselves at danger to save you without a moment's hesitation.

And I had apparently made one more of those friends in the last few days. I had let Andrew guide me to a picnic table after climbing through the window, but when I saw Kristofer leaning heavily on Michelle's arm, I got up at once to run to his side.

"I'm okay," he said, although he was looking decidedly gray. "I just tweaked my knee again, is all."

From the way he was putting so much of his weight on Michelle, I suspected his tweak was going to need surgical correction, or at the very least a ton more physical therapy, but I didn't argue. I just waited until he had both feet on solid ground outside the café before pulling him into a tight hug.

"Thank you for the rescue," I said.

"Well," he said, and the subsequent blush brought a little needed color to his cheeks. "It was nothing."

"Has anyone called the police?" Loke asked.

"We did," Jessica said. "They should be here any minute."

"Sadly, Ingrid and I can't spare a moment to answer all their questions," Loke said. "We have another emergency. One that we had agreed we'd deal with first."

"What?" I asked at his sharp look. "I didn't *choose* to come here instead."

"Didn't you?" he asked.

"If you need to go, you should go," Michelle said. "You two shouty people both seem to be a bit deaf at the moment, so I guess you don't hear the sirens. We've got this without you, but you need to scram."

"Doorway?" I said to Loke. I couldn't remember the last time I had felt so exhausted. And I still had a magical battle to fight. Who knew when I'd find a moment to rest?

"Doorway," Loke said.

It was almost a comfort that he sounded as worn out as I felt. The two of us ducked back inside the café and disappeared just as the first police car pulled into the gravel lot outside.

CHAPTER TWENTY-TWO

Loke and I emerged from the mobile home doorway with a loud slap as that flimsy door crashed against the thin exterior wall yet again.

Not that I really noticed. The pillar of magical light streaming up into the sky was impossible to miss now. It was, in fact, blinding.

And my ears were still ringing from the gunfire. I was feeling disconnected from the world around me, and not in a good way.

"You see that, right?" Loke said close to my ear.

"Yeah. So do you?" I asked.

"I didn't yesterday when you did that drawing, but I definitely do now," he said. "This isn't good."

"Please tell me Mormor isn't draining power from the protective spells around Villmark and throwing them up into the sky," I said, biting at my lip hard enough to draw blood.

Loke squinted up into the pillar of magic for a moment, but then to my immense relief, he shook his head.

"No, this is new power," he said.

"Are you sure? I've never actually sensed the protective spell around Villmark. Not directly, anyway," I admitted.

"I sense it every time I pass through it," he said with more confidence. "This isn't that."

"So maybe this isn't so disastrous as it looks?" I said hopefully.

But he was shaking his head in sorrow. "No, I have a feeling this being so close is why Villmark shut down. It's protecting itself. Even if we find a way to get this to stop, who says we'll be able to find a way to open Villmark up again? Is there anyone on the inside who could even try to help?"

"Kara?" I said. Loke didn't argue the point, but we both knew she was too new with her powers to be any real help.

"There you are," Jesús said as he walked up to us. We were still standing at the bottom of the mobile home stairs, and he had left his sister by the hall doors to join us. She was talking on a cellphone, or trying to. Runde's bad reception was working against her, and even with one finger plugged in her opposite ear, it was clear she was having a hard time hearing anything.

"Who's she talking to?" I asked.

"Her mentor back in Duluth. There isn't time for her to get here, but Tlalli thinks she can get inside without her. With your help, of course," he said, looking at both Loke and me.

I nodded, gripped the strap on my art bag, and crossed the parking lot just as Tlalli was putting her phone away. She gave me a tentative smile.

"You have thoughts?" I said.

"It's not as bad as I feared," she said. "You see the mix of colors at the borders, right? The way the different colored threads are braided together?"

I had to shake my head regretfully. Tlalli sucked her teeth in frustration and looked up into the sky.

But to my surprise, it was Loke who said, "Celtic magic, right? The braids and colors thing, I mean."

"That's right," Tlalli said slowly.

"Yeah, that's just a perception thing, then," he said. Then he turned to me. "You see the bind runes."

"Well, not at the moment, but in my sketch, sure," I said.

"Right. It's just two ways of seeing the same nonvisible thing," he said.

"But what does it mean?" I asked.

"Well, for me, it would mean that how I bring this pillar down is to unravel the braid work," Tlalli said.

"And you can unbind the runes," Loke said to me.

"How exactly am I supposed to do that?" I asked.

Loke rolled his eyes then jabbed at my art bag.

"You want me to *draw* them apart?" I asked, still confused.

"With your wand, not your pencil, but yeah," he said.

"Oh, like you did when we were on the lake trying to find the shore," Tlalli said.

I frowned, but then I remembered that day. We had been lost in a storm trying to find a house on the shore at Thunder Bay. Some sort of being that was part of the lake or under the lake—or, my worst fear, actually *was* the lake—had been working pretty hard to drown us.

But I had drawn in the air with my finger, and that act had invoked magic that I, at that point, had barely understood.

I had never done it again. Once I had started learning the runes, and then acquired my wand, such basic, instinctual magic just didn't come to mind first when I was trying to solve problems.

But it had been effective at the time. And I was so much stronger now.

"I can try," I said at last. "How do you unravel the braid work?" I asked Tlalli.

"You'll see my hands moving," she said, miming undoing a braid. "But it's through magic, really. I don't know if I'll see what you're doing, or if you'll see me, but I think the two of us together will sense that we're achieving something or not."

"And we already tried just knocking on the door," Jesús said. "In case anyone was wondering."

"Let's get to it, then," I said, and took my bag off my shoulder. I still had my wand in the back waistband of my jeans, but I didn't want to try working with my bag encumbering me. I shoved it into Loke's arms, and he took it with a huff of breath.

I rolled my eyes at him. It wasn't *that* heavy.

Then I half-closed my eyes and opened up my magic senses. The pillar of power was extremely hard to tune out. It was like standing under a rocket perpetually in the middle of taking off, a constant explosion of crackling sound and burning light, and even a magical sort of blistering heat.

But with a little focus, I could move all that to my background awareness. And then I could sense my grandmother, still working to bring all that power down.

She was so very tired.

But she was okay. I shifted my awareness again, away from her and back to that pillar. I had to concentrate before I could make out the bind runes. They were so very tiny. But I used my wand to draw a circle around one, then draw it down closer to me until it was floating over the palm of my hand.

This wasn't like the bluetooth symbol at all. That was two runes overlapping each other, a sort of bind rune that was often used by someone wanting to sign something with their initials. Given the situation, it wasn't entirely surprising that what I was looking at was more complicated than that.

No, what it looked like was a snowflake, a six-pointed form where each of the six points was a different rune. Not surprisingly, it was constructed from runes I hadn't studied yet with Haraldr. But I recognized the forms from my art. I could sound out the letters, if that were important.

But I also had a gut sense that all these runes put together were working to create a very strong protective ward.

I immediately opened my eyes, rocking back on my heels with a gasp as the sudden shift from the magical world to the mundane one knocked me for a momentary loop.

"Ingrid!" Loke said, moving to catch me. But I didn't fall. I caught my balance, then lunged to grab Tlalli's arm.

"Stop!" I said to her. "Don't take them apart! Tlalli!"

Then she was the one gasping for air as her eyes flew open. "They are protective spells!" she said.

"I know!" I said.

"We can't take them down. They are all that's holding all this together," she said.

"I think it's my grandmother's work," I said. "She's creating them to contain the power inside that pillar. But it's all she can do. And she's at the end of her strength."

"We need to get inside," Tlalli said. "But how?"

We heard the gritty sound of footsteps approaching across the parking lot and saw Andrew, Jessica, Michelle and Kristofer coming towards us. Kristofer was still limping badly, and the others were walking slowly to accommodate his pace.

"That was fast," Loke said, looking towards the top of the bluff and the café just out of sight.

"Too fast," I grumbled. "We need to get inside. Now. But how do we get rid of Kristofer?"

"I can try to run interference," Jesús said doubtfully.

"We can just ask Michelle to take him out of here," Loke whispered to me as the foursome drew into earshot.

"I'm going to take a look at the back door," Tlalli said, then left before I could tell her that it wouldn't make any difference.

"Melissa is in custody, and we finally got a hold of Heather. She's okay," Jessica told me.

"What's going on here?" Kristofer asked.

"Nothing. We're just… locked out," I said lamely.

"Where's your grandmother?" Andrew asked.

"Inside?" I said.

"Is she okay?" Jessica asked. She pulled at the door handles, but the doors wouldn't open.

"Yeah, she just can't hear us knocking, I guess," I said. I tried to signal Andrew and Jessica with my eyes that I needed Kristofer to go before I could say anything, but they weren't looking at me. They were kind of avoiding my eyes, I realized. Which was frustrating. But also weird.

"Is there a spare key?" Michelle asked. Jessica had stepped back after trying the door handles, and now Kristofer was standing right in front of them. But he appeared to be examining the crack between the doors.

"It's not locked really," Jessica said. "The handles open just fine. But there's something on the inside blocking the doors from opening."

"I can see it," Kristofer said from where he was bent over, peering between the doors. He had gotten one to swing just a little ways open, increasing the gap enough to peer through with one eye. "It looks like a stick of some kind. Like a broom or a mop handle."

"You don't look so hot," I said to him, which was conveniently true. He was still quite gray.

"He didn't want to sit down," Michelle said apologetically. "His danger sense is tingling or something."

"His what now?" I asked.

"I thought it was you being held at gunpoint that was making the hairs on the back of my neck stand up, only it didn't go away after that woman was taken away by the police," Kristofer said. He had straightened up from looking through the door and was checking all of his pockets for something.

"He insisted we get down here to check on you," Michelle said with an apologetic look.

"Oh, no worries," I said. I hoped that Kristofer would interpret that as meaning "I'm okay," but Michelle would hear, "I understand why you brought someone who doesn't know the secret of Villmark into the middle of a big secret of Villmark mess."

But I'm not sure if that actually came across or not.

"Try this," Loke said, and produced a long-bladed knife out of nowhere. I had actually seen it before. He had used it to fight a monstrous white wolf that had fallen out of the sky when we were in the wilds outside of Villmark one time.

Kristofer took it and slid the blade in the gap between the doors. It took a bit of fiddling, but then we all heard the sound of a wooden handle falling to the tile floor. It was only as he turned to hand the knife back to Loke that he even noticed what he held in his hand.

"Did you get this from the Renaissance Festival?" he asked as he examined the blade and then the hilt. "It looks Viking."

"Something like that," Loke said as he took his knife back and promptly disappeared it again.

Tlalli was just coming back around the corner of the building with a defeated shake of her head as Michelle pushed both the doors open. Then the eight of us went in to the dark interior of the meeting hall.

The meeting hall, not the mead hall. My grandmother had managed to bring down at least some of the spells, then. Although with a quick blink into magical awareness, I saw a lot of them were still tangled in the kind of knots you only get when untangling gets too frustrating and you start pulling too hard at everything.

How were we ever going to fix this?

"Well, this is all wrong," Kristofer said.

"What do you mean?" I asked. From his point of view, everything was just as it should be. The little general store lacked only someone at the register to be complete, and all the chairs in the bar area were neatly arranged under the tables. It looked like all we needed to do was turn on the lights and we'd be open for business.

"This isn't what it looked like when I was here before," Kristofer said, looking from one to another of us as if afraid he sounded crazy.

"Sorry, man. I wasn't here before," Jesús said with a shrug. A lie, but he was just trying to be helpful.

"It was like your knife," Kristofer insisted, pointing at Loke. "It looked all… Viking. And I'm not talking about football."

"How much were you drinking?" Loke asked.

"I had *a* beer," Kristofer said. "I had work in the morning. But it wasn't just that night. I remember coming here once in high school, and it was the same. I don't know how decorations can change a place so much, but it didn't look like this. It looked like a Viking hall. But someone else on the team told the coach I was out drinking, and I got in so much trouble I never tried to come back again. But you know what I mean, right?"

Jessica and Andrew both avoided his questioning eyes, but Michelle gave me a pained look.

"Go ahead," I said to her, and she gave me such a relieved smile that any trepidation I had about that decision just evaporated.

"You're totally right," she told him, putting a hand on his arm. "This place can look like a Viking hall when Ingrid's grandmother wants it to. That's what you saw. You aren't crazy."

His relieved smile was like Michelle's turned up to ten times the wattage. Luckily, it wasn't aimed at me. It was all for Michelle.

"How's your danger sense now?" I asked him.

He put a hand on the back of his neck as if checking in with the hair there. "Still tingling?" he said.

"Mormor," I said, and nodded at Tlalli. We both headed to the cellar door behind the bar. I was vaguely aware of Loke stepping up behind me to block Kristofer from following, but couldn't make out just what he said to get the former hockey player to stand down.

We found my grandmother in the middle of the room at the bottom of the stairs. She was still on her feet, but only because the majority of her weight was on her staff. She was leaning on it so heavily she was practically draped over it. But her lips were still moving, whispering spells over and over again.

"Nora, let go now," Tlalli said as she put her arm around my grandmother's shoulders.

And just like that, my grandmother let go, of magic and standing upright both. Her staff fell with a clatter, and it was all Tlalli could do to guide her over to sit on the bottom step of the staircase.

I immediately lunged into my grandmother's place and looked up, wand in hand. I was in the very heart of the pillar of power now, the source of it. I reached out to gather up what my grandmother had been grasping before anything could slip away.

It was a lot.

"You have to relax," I heard Tlalli say. At first, I thought she was talking to my grandmother. But then I felt her hands on my shoulders and her mouth close to my ear, whispering. "You have to relax. Just slowly let the tension go. The spells are running in an ever-tightening protective loop. Don't let it go all at once. Just… gently."

I realized what she meant. That was what all the bind runes were about. They were there to contain the leaking power, but they were also feeding the leaking power. And the power itself was fighting to escape.

It was like if a net full of fish all swam in the same direction at once. No net would ever be strong enough to contain them. My grandmother had been fighting a losing battle.

I loosened that magical net enough to give the fishlike power a little more room to expand and move. Then, once its frantic panic died down, I started pulling it back in again.

But slowly.

"I'm going to take down a few of the protective binds, but not all of them," Tlalli said to me as her hands left my shoulders. "You just keep doing what you're doing."

I gave her a nod, but didn't trust myself to speak. It was like I was trying to keep my awareness focused on a million independent things at once, and I didn't dare lose track of any of them.

Then I heard a voice singing. It took a minute for my tired brain to grasp that I was hearing Old Norse, a language that has as much to do with modern Villmarker as Latin does to Spanish.

But once I knew what I was hearing, I realized it was one of the old rune poems. I didn't know any of them had ever been set to music.

But the flow of the melody aided Tlalli and me in our work. We flowed with it, and the power flowed through us.

It wasn't fast work by any means, but eventually we came to the end of it.

And the mead hall was once more just as it should be. Currently, in the daytime, a perfectly ordinary meeting space in a small town in northern Minnesota.

I turned to see my grandmother resting on the bottom of the steps, her back to the stone wall. She finished the last verse of the old song, her voice cracking in exhaustion but a glow of contentment on her face. Then she stopped with a smile.

"Good to see you again, Tlalli," she said. "Would you like to come to a wedding?"

CHAPTER TWENTY-THREE

Despite my grandmother's optimistic words to Tlalli, it was all the two of us could do to get her back upstairs again. We got her settled into a chair at a table near the bar and she slumped down into it gratefully.

"I just need a minute," she said, propping her elbows on the table and resting her forehead on her hands.

"A minute to do what?" Loke asked, a little too eagerly.

"A minute to rest before I walk the rest of the way to my bed," she said. "Have a heart, Loke Grímsson. I've been awake and working high level magic for the better part of two days."

"Of course," he said, with better grace than I would've expected from him.

"Do you want me to try drawing Esja again?" I asked.

"No," he said, and summoned up a smile completely unlike his usual leering grin. "I feel like she's probably okay. But I'll see her tomorrow, right?"

"Tomorrow," my grandmother agreed, still not looking up.

"So you've already tried—?" I started to say.

"The minute I felt the spells drop back down," he said. "Nothing."

"Tomorrow, I promise you," my grandmother said.

"I feel like I shouldn't ask, but I'm curious about what we're talking about," Kristofer said.

My grandmother lifted her head at his voice and peered at him closely. Then she glanced over at Michelle, even though Michelle was way across the room speaking with Jessica in low tones.

"So, it's you. I was starting to think I'd never see you inside these walls again. Well, you probably guessed that half of the patrons of my hall don't come from Runde," my grandmother said to Kristofer.

"That makes sense," he said, but from the look on his face, he hadn't guessed anything of the sort.

"They come from a village nearby, the descendants of a lost colony of Viking era settlers. They are hidden from most of the modern world, although this hall is one of the places they can go. We're currently cut off from them, but that will all be sorted in the morning." Then she gave him a brilliant smile and said, "Would you like to come to a wedding? I believe Michelle still lacks a date."

"Nora!" Michelle gasped, having overheard at least that much of the conversation.

"Well, I *am* free," he said. "And I've always loved weddings."

"You knew he could see through the spells?" I asked my grandmother.

"Yes. There are always a few who can see through magic, even magic as powerful as mine," she said. "He's not the only one, by any means. But I can sense the presence of one such when they're in my hall, and I keep an eye out for them afterward just to be sure they handle it appropriately."

"What would be inappropriate?" Loke wondered, but my grandmother ignored him.

"You've been here exactly twice," she said to Kristofer. "Once as a teenager, for which I'm sorry I arranged a bit of trouble to keep you from coming back again. Teenagers are notoriously unlikely to behave *appropriately*," she said with a supercilious glance Loke's way. "But I can see you've grown into a man of trust and discretion. I don't need to worry about you keeping our secrets. Do I?"

That last sounded a lot like a threat. But Kristofer just swallowed hard before saying, "Yes, ma'am. I mean, no, ma'am. I mean, you can count on me."

She smiled and nodded and looked like she wanted to push up from the table. But after trying to leverage herself up with her arms didn't yield much movement, she slumped back into the chair with a sigh.

"So I guess you caught Melissa Scott in the act of... something," Loke said to me.

"She was putting arsenic in the flour and sugar supplies," I said. Then I glanced up to make sure Jessica was listening. "Jessica, you're going to have to throw out everything in the café and give the whole place a thorough cleaning before it will be safe to open again. I'm sorry we didn't figure out what was happening sooner."

"How could you? None of us even knew who this Melissa woman was, let alone what she was after," Jessica said. She was hugging herself as she spoke, and her gaze didn't lift any higher than my feet.

"I can come through to check everything before you open," my grandmother offered. "I'm sure you'll handle it all wonderfully, but a little extra peace of mind isn't a bad thing."

"I'd appreciate that, Nora. Thank you," Jessica said. But she still seemed so down, strangely sad in a way I couldn't put my finger on.

"Is something else the matter?" I asked, moving closer to her so that I wasn't trying to make my voice carry across the room.

"It's Heather," she said.

"What happened to Heather?" I rushed to ask.

"Oh, nothing! She's fine!" Jessica assured me, so flustered she actually looked up at me for a second before dropping her eyes back down to the floor. "It's just... she's decided not to stay in Runde after all. I have no idea where she'll go next. I have a feeling she doesn't want to tell me."

"I can see how that's crummy timing, just when you have so much extra work to do to get your café open again, but you know we're all there to help you, right?" I said.

"Oh, I know I can rely on all you guys for help," Jessica assured me. "It's just, I'm sorry that I didn't succeed in helping her out."

"Maybe you did," Andrew said. "Maybe everything that happened in the last few days, as terrible as it's been, has been a life-changing experience for her."

"Hopefully in a good way," Loke said drily. "Not in a villain back-story kind of way."

I shot him a furious glare, but he blithely ignored me.

"You know none of what happened was ever your fault," I said to Jessica. "Melissa was crazy, and no one is to blame for what happened except her. And you were never even the intended victim. She had you confused with Heather. Not that Heather had done anything to Melissa either. No, everything that happened was the end result of things that really only existed in Melissa's messed up imagination."

"It's just as well she's gone then, isn't it? No one needs a Doppel-gänger around," Loke said. "Especially one who wants to steal your boyfriends."

"I would have to have a boyfriend for someone to steal my boyfriend," Jessica muttered to the floor.

"Same," Michelle said, taking a step so that her body was between Loke and Jessica. She even had her hands up, halfway curled into fists, as if she were willing to fight to prove that point.

Loke took a big breath. I had no idea what he was about to say. I was just absolutely certain that no one in the room wanted to hear it. I one-upped Michelle by stepping right into Loke's face and glared up at him with my fiercest glower.

I'd like to think it had a little extra warning in it, like I was reminding him that while Michelle's fists might not be particularly frightening, my magic certainly could be.

He lifted an eyebrow at me, unimpressed.

But then my grandmother said, "Loke, come help an old woman to her feet."

He smirked at me, then turned away to do her bidding.

The most mind-blowing part of the entire exchange, though, had to be my grandmother referring to herself as an old woman. Mostly I think she said it to grab Loke's attention.

But partly, I think she was starting to feel her age. Or some of it, anyway.

I decided to chalk it up to her exhaustion, only temporary, and went to help Loke get my grandmother to her feet.

"Ingrid, Jessica says her mother is still out of town, so there is room at her house for Jesús and I to stay the night," Tlalli said.

"Oh, fantastic!" I said. Because of course there was no room for them in the mobile home.

"So we'll meet in the cavern behind the waterfall in the morning?" she said.

"Nine o'clock sharp," my grandmother said. Her voice was strong and steady despite the way she was putting most of her weight on Loke and me.

"You're in for a treat," Michelle said to Kristofer as the rest of them followed us out the meeting hall doors. Andrew was the last one out, and as I glanced back, I saw him immediately turn to test the doors again after they shut behind him. But they opened with ease. He turned away, then saw me watching him over my shoulder. He flushed, sketched a little wave goodbye, then ran to catch up with Jessica and the Rodríguez siblings.

Loke and I got my grandmother up the rickety steps into her mobile home, but after that point she shook our hands away and proceeded on her own down the hall to her bedroom. She made extensive use of the walls of the narrow corridor to keep herself upright, but she still got to her door under her own steam.

"I will see you both in the morning, well-rested and ready for work," she said to us before closing the door behind her.

"Well-rested?" Loke whispered to me. "What exactly does she think we're going to be up all night doing? Finding more murders to solve?"

"Pillow fights," I said. "You know, I don't want to kill you, but I wouldn't mind hurting you somewhat severely for making trouble just now."

"What? What did I do?" he said with feigned innocence.

"You don't need to make cracks about anybody's lack of boyfriends," I hissed at him, trying my best to keep my voice down so my grandmother could rest. It was challenging. The walls were paper thin, and I was highly annoyed.

"In case you haven't been paying attention, everyone basically *has* boyfriends," he hissed back at me. Then he smirked. "Present company possibly excluded. But that's entirely your own fault."

"What the heck are you talking about?" I demanded.

With a nervous look down the corridor, he grabbed my arm and steered me to the now-familiar battered couch under the front window. It was as far away as we could get without actually going outside.

"I'll grant you, you missed some stuff when you were chatting with Melissa," he said.

"Chatting," I repeated. "Not the word I'd use for it."

"Whatever," he said, waving his hand as if swatting my response away. "Look, after you didn't join the rest of us coming back from Duluth, and you weren't still *in* Duluth, I went to the restaurant."

"You went to the restaurant? No wonder it took you so long to turn up," I said. "I thought for sure once you didn't find me in Duluth, you'd go back to the café."

"Why would I go there?" he asked, his brows furrowed together in puzzlement.

"Because it was the last place we were before we went to Duluth?" I said.

"Oh," he said, and blinked. "Yeah, that makes sense."

"Yes, it does," I agreed. "Why did the restaurant make more sense to you at the time?"

"Because Andrew, Jessica and Michelle were almost definitely there, and if you weren't with me, you were probably with them," he said with a shrug. "Look, you're the one who picked your own doorway. I didn't shove you off my path."

"I didn't—" I started to protest, but then decided to drop it. Whatever had happened in that moment, I was going to want to try replicating a few times before I decided I understood it. Maybe I didn't need Loke to do the doorway trick anymore. Maybe I had intuitively worked it out and could do it on my own now.

But testing that would have to wait for later.

I sighed and asked, "What did I miss in the restaurant, then?"

"Well, I was partly right. The three of them were there. But so was Kristofer," he said. He propped his arm on the back of the couch, clutching his wrist with his other hand, and leaning forward like a gossip eager to dish. "He was already talking about his sense of danger tingling or however he said it. He was very worried."

"Well, I *was* in danger," I said.

"Yeah, but the reason he had gotten out of bed without any sleep and rushed to the restaurant and not the café was because he was afraid it was *Michelle* that was in danger," Loke said. "When I came in, he had just come in the door all frantic and worried about Michelle. And Michelle was all confused on a couple of levels. But I could tell Anna knew the score."

"Kristofer is still crushing on Michelle then," I said. "Or crushing again, maybe. That doesn't make him her boyfriend."

"Give it a week," he said, but then he waved his hand as if erasing those words from a blackboard. "No, two days. Because tomorrow is a wedding, and he loves weddings." He rolled his eyes dramatically at the word "loves."

"Okay," I said slowly, because that all sounded way too feasible. "But that still leaves Jessica."

"You're going to call me out on a technicality again?" he asked.

"You're not exactly explaining yourself," I said.

"Heather wasn't subtle when she was going after Andrew right in front of our very eyes," he said.

"Heather is nuts," I said. Which was way too dismissive, and I felt bad as soon as the words were out. I tried again. "I don't think Heather's targeting was any better than Melissa's."

"Let's spell it out for you then," Loke said, that grin of pure delight back on his face. "Jessica changed her look, for reasons that seem to completely baffle you. But you can at least allow that something new came into her life that made her feel differently about her appearance. Does that seem fair?"

"Okay," I agreed. "I've not been in Runde for a while. Maybe it was a slower transition than it seemed to me."

"Meh?" Loke said, but didn't explain that little noise before going on. "Jessica also feels like she needs to make up for something she's done or is doing or—and I'm voting for option three—hasn't even done but really wants to and is self-flagellating in advance. Because that's just who she is."

"I do keep hearing about her karma," was as much as I was willing to concede.

"And she wanted to talk to you about it," he said. He raised a hand to forestall my objection. "Trust me. This is exactly what she wanted to talk to you about. Alone. Not in the mead hall. It wasn't ever about Dave or Heather."

"Do you think she still wants to talk to me?" I asked him.

"Obviously," he said, rolling his eyes again. "Why do you think she can't quite look at you? She's still waiting to talk to you. But don't try running over there now. She has a house full of guests."

"Right," I said. "This murder investigation really derailed a lot of mundane and yet important stuff."

"Tell me about it," he said.

"I still don't see how all that adds up to…" I started to say.

But then I did see it. The gipt rune I kept drawing in the café, the one that wasn't touching in the middle. The way both of them had been avoiding looking at me since I'd come back to town. It all made sense.

Including Loke's absolute delight. He couldn't be happier if he had created the entire circumstance himself, manipulating us all like dolls in a dollhouse.

And still, there was no way to keep him from talking. "I mean," he said, leaning back so he could more effectively look down at me. "Why do you think Andrew has been trying so very hard to ship you with anyone at all?"

"Because—" I started to say, but Loke just couldn't let me finish.

"Because he needs to know you're okay before he can do anything about his own feelings. And so does Jessica. And those poor kids. Because you are so very dense."

Then he turned away from me, extending both of his arms high into the air. It was almost a victory salute, but then at the last second, he retracted them to fold his hands behind his head.

But the smug look lingered. And it's not like I could blame him.

I knew he was right about everything.

CHAPTER TWENTY-FOUR

AT PRECISELY NINE the next morning, we all gathered behind the mead hall and made a rather posh-looking procession hiking up the trail beside the river and up the side of the bluff to the cavern behind the waterfall.

Well, mostly posh. My grandmother was wearing her full volva outfit of deep purple and sky blue, the full skirt whispering around her calves as she walked. And the Runde folks were looking good in summer dresses and brightly colored shirts and ties.

Even Tlalli and Jesús had gotten dressed up, although it had required an early morning trip back to Duluth via the mobile home door courtesy of Loke. Jesús was dressed much like Andrew and Kristofer, in slacks and a button-up shirt, although his tie was a bolo tie that looked handcrafted: a gorgeous piece of turquoise set in brightly polished silver.

But Tlalli was stunning in a traditional Mexican dress of deep rose red trimmed with white lace. Her skirt was even fuller than my grandmother's, and the color against the brown of her skin was just gorgeous. She even had a rose in her hair where it was pulled back on the left side.

I doubted Loke would ever look any different from he did in that moment. Black tunic and black leggings with black boots was pretty much his forever look. Even for a wedding. Even at Midsummer. So it wasn't odd that he didn't look like he felt out of place.

But me? Well, I had showered, at least. But I was still wearing the same thing I had been wearing for the last three days. Jeans I had been crawling around on basement floors and attic rooms over garages in, a very pitted out T-shirt, and a sun shirt that was as wrinkled as a twelve-year-old's gym uniform at the end of a year being stuffed inside a tiny locker.

I really hoped my grandmother could get us inside the Villmark protective barrier in a hurry. If I didn't have time to run home and change before the ceremony, I was going to be deeply unhappy.

"Everyone, please wait here for a moment," my grandmother said when we were in the cavern behind the waterfall. Her voice carried easily despite the crashing of the water, and I knew she was magically oomphing it again. "Ingrid, Tlalli and I are going to open the door, and then we'll all go through together." Then she gave Tlalli and me a quick nod, and we followed her down the currently dead-ending cave.

Loke, of course, followed. Even if my grandmother's magic voice had been set to give commands that had to be obeyed, in my experience, Loke was immune to that sort of thing. So I doubted she had even tried.

"I can feel it," Tlalli said, running her fingertips over the stone of the cave wall. "It's retracting. Kind of like an injured creature curling into a fetal position. It's all defensive."

"Yes," my grandmother agreed. "We just need to let it know it's safe now. Then it will relax, and we'll be able to pass through it like before."

"How do we do that?" Tlalli asked.

And my grandmother turned to look at me.

"I don't know what to do," I said.

"You've been to the ancestral fire," she said.

"I can't get back there," I said.

"You don't have to. You just have to reach out to it and tell it everything is okay," she said. "Tlalli and I will back you up."

Then she reached out a hand to each of us. I took her hand in one of mine, then reached out to Tlalli with the other. The three of us stood in a tight circle, heads bowed as we shifted our focus.

I was just aware of Loke behind me, folding his arms as he leaned back against the cave wall to watch. Then I tuned him out too and reached out for the fire.

I could sense it at once. It was, after all, just on the other side of the cave wall before me that wasn't even supposed to be a wall. It was supposed to be an opening.

When my grandmother had said "ancestral fire," I had assumed she meant the true fire, the ancient one I had found quite by accident deep within the cave complex below Villmark. I never would've found it without Mjolner guiding my way. And I wasn't in a hurry to try looking for it again. Its power had been overwhelming. No, it had been *scary*.

But the fire that always burned just behind the waterfall was familiar. It didn't have the power of the older fire, but it did have a stronger bond with the people of Villmark as they existed today. The Thors and their father, and Kara and Nilda, all took turns guarding that fire, ensuring that its flames never died. And Kara had first discovered her own volva powers while staring into its flames.

That fire hadn't been used to create the bubble that protected the original settlers of Villmark, but it was in tune with it and with the people of Villmark both.

And it was the source of the fear that had locked down the protections.

I had pictured a long process, like those internet videos of rescue workers coaxing traumatized animals out of hiding places so they could be taken to veterinarian hospitals. I figured I'd need to offer something like food, always keeping my personal vibe calming, and be prepared to be infinitely patient.

Instead, it was like coming home to a puppy who had missed you so very much while you were at the grocery store. The minute that ancestral fire sensed my presence, I was overwhelmed with feelings of happy welcome and abundant relief.

Like a puppy, that fire had thought it would never, ever see me again. And the wave after wave of warm feeling it was washing over me was a lot. Like the exuberant licks of a puppy.

I opened my eyes with a laugh and saw my grandmother and Tlalli grinning as well.

"I guess you were missed," Tlalli said even as the stone wall behind her faded away to become the sandy-floored mouth of a deeper cave.

Loke just turned to whistle loudly back over his shoulder to summon the others, then pushed past the three of us to be the first into Villmark.

And was immediately bowled over by a charging horde of Thors. They were in their leather armor with weapons brandished, and their eyes were half-crazed with berserker energy. My grandmother yelped and grabbed Tlalli to pull her out of the way, but I stood my ground.

"Valkissons!" I cried. My voice rang out, echoing through the tiny cave. And it wasn't even magically amplified. Thoralv with his spiky hair and curved knives and Thormund with his thick braids and spear the size of a railroad tie were passing to either side of me, and I had a momentary panic that they were going to attack the wedding guests before I could properly get their attention.

But I needn't have worried. Because Thorbjorn had been right behind them, and the minute he saw me standing there, he dropped his axe at my feet and reached out to snatch both of them by the backs of their collars. He grunted as he dragged them to a halt, and then again when Thorge and Thorulv crashed into his back.

For one chaotic moment, there was a lot of shouting and shoving, two brothers trying to break free of Thorbjorn's grasp while two more attempted to push past him. The whole time, Thorbjorn just grinned down at me with an energy a lot like the ancestral fire.

Didn't think he'd see me again. Probably wished he could jump all over me and lick my face. That sort of thing.

And I just grinned back up at him like an idiot.

"I think we can all settle down now, right? We're clearly not under attack. It's just Ingrid and Nora." I heard Kara speak those words before she pushed into view, her sister at her side. They were also in full armor, although Kara had put her sword away already, and Nilda was in the process of doing so. Kara touched Thorge and Thorulv on their shoulders and they promptly stopped trying to plow their brother over.

"We didn't know what was happening," Thorulv, the oldest of the Thors, said to my grandmother as he sheathed both his swords. "When the barrier locked down, we just assumed there was an attack about to break through."

"It was a little worrying when even Loke didn't seem able to get back inside," Kara said.

My grandmother was about to speak when Loke groaned loudly then staggered back to his feet. "I have to get home. I have to see Esja," he said. Although he looked a little out of it, like he had hit his head on something on the way down. But Nilda grabbed his arm before he got far.

"She's not there, Loke," she said.

"What? Where is she?" he asked, eyes wide with fright.

"Like I said, we were worried when you didn't come back. So Nilda and I went to your house and brought Esja into town," Kara told him. "She's at Sigvin's house. They've been keeping each other company through what, honestly, has probably been the longest three days in any of our lives."

"You didn't think we'd be back?" I asked her. But I was looking up at Thorbjorn.

"We weren't sure," Nilda said.

"I didn't know what to do if you couldn't get through," Kara said.

"I knew you'd get through," Thorbjorn said to me. "And so did Mjolner."

I was just about to ask him where Mjolner was when I saw my cat's head pop up over Thorbjorn's shoulder. Mjolner was tucked inside a pouch that rested on Thorbjorn's shoulder like a quiver.

"You were going to bring my cat into battle?" I asked him.

"You try telling him it's a bad idea," Thorbjorn grumbled. Mjolner meowed loudly. Then Thorbjorn flinched as Mjolner dug his claws in to leap from his perch on Thorbjorn's shoulder to my arms.

I caught him and held him tight. He butted his head under my chin over and over again. Not quite puppy love, but I would take it.

I was home.

CHAPTER TWENTY-FIVE

THE NEXT HOUR or so was beyond frantic. As worried as I had been about my clothing, the rest of the wedding party had been in battle gear waiting by the fire for the last three days, so at least I was one shower up on them.

Loke made a beeline for Sigvin's house, leaving the rest of us behind the minute we emerged from the caves and into the meadow that overlooked Lake Superior. Nilda and Kara weren't far behind him, already undoing their tight braids as they fast-walked into town.

Four of the Thors had started working overtime teasing the fifth, Thorge, about his upcoming nuptials. Although the second youngest of them, he was the first to get married, and I sensed they had been holding back a lot of the traditional joking over the last few days. All that pent up jocularity was pouring out all at once, and I pitied poor, overwhelmed Thorge.

Mjolner's claws were digging deep into my clothing, but I had no intention of setting him down until I absolutely had to. He was still clinging to me in a tight, purring ball when I parted ways with the others at the village commons, heading to my own front gate just a few houses south on the main road.

My grandmother was bringing our Runde and Duluth guests up to the commons to mingle with the locals. I just caught a glimpse of Tlalli spinning her skirt and smiling up at Roarr of all people before I had to leave that all behind to rush into my house and change.

Tlalli had met Roarr once before. He had been with us when Loke and I had been to her apartment the first time. And she had been fascinated by this strange, tall Scandinavian who had never had Mexican food before in his life. But now she was in an entire village of such men.

I supposed she was only chatting with Roarr because he was familiar.

Or rather, I hoped.

I went up to my bedroom and, claw by claw, pulled a very reluctant Mjolner off my shoulder. Luckily, I had left my volva gown out before heading to Runde three days before. The alternating sections of red and green didn't look quite as good on me as the rose red color of Tlalli's gown looked on her, but it did bring out the green in my eyes. The long white sleeves that reached down to the ground were going to make eating interesting. I would have to be extra careful.

I tucked my bronze wand into the loop of my belt, but only because it belonged there. I didn't seriously think I was going to need it.

Then I finished everything off by pinning the emerald-eyed cat brooch to my breast. It had once belonged to my grandmother's grandmother, a fact that had meant little to me the last time I had worn it, but more now that I had actually met that woman.

Being a volva was an endless string of strange experiences. But the strangest of all was probably how easily I was getting used to it.

Then I went downstairs, Mjolner still close at my heels, and wrapped the now-dry painting that was my gift to the happy couple. Whatever tweaks I might have wanted to make, I had to let it go now.

But I was sure they were going to love it anyway.

I reached the village commons to find the rest of the wedding party already gathered there. It was time.

We had made it home just in time.

The ceremony was brief, as was the Villmarker way. But the party would last all through the shortest night of the year and into the next day. And everyone was anxious to get the drinking, dining and dancing started.

Once dinner was served, I would be stuck at the main table for hours, so after the ceremony ended, I headed out into the rows of smaller tables to catch up with my other friends first.

Loke had changed into another, albeit slightly finer, black outfit. He didn't see me looking his way, intent as he was in fussing over his sister. But Esja saw me and gave me a little wave and something almost like an eye roll in the direction of her brother. I laughed but didn't dare interrupt their moment.

But she was looking good. She had more color to her cheeks than usual, and they even looked a little rounder, like someone had managed to get some real food into her. The last few days might've been stressful for her, but Sigvin and her family had looked after her well.

And Loke clearly appreciated it, because he was letting Sigvin sit on the other side of him. He was even listening as she chatted with him about something, and offered her the smallest of smiles at something she said.

Loke, not fleeing at the mere sight of Sigvin. And the world hadn't even had to end first.

Tlalli and Jesús were sitting together at one of the tables, chatting with a group of Villmarkers that included a surprisingly engaged Roarr. Not only was he looking at people when he was talking to them, but he was even smiling. Rarely and briefly, but still. It was a big change from his usual demeanor.

I was still looking for my Runde friends when the band struck up a song in a burst of drums that sent a roar through the crowd. I didn't know the song myself, but it was apparently quite a popular one, and many Villmarker couples started pulling each other towards the dance area.

It was a catchy tune. I was bobbing my head to the beat as I walked when I finally found Andrew sitting alone at a table staring off into space.

But when I followed the line of his thousand-yard stare, Jessica was just off the center of it. Like he was barely able to not just gaze at her.

I sighed. I really hated it when Loke was right. But Loke was right. I needed to fix this.

"Hey," I said, snapping Andrew out of his reverie.

"Oh. Hey. Nice ceremony," he said, rubbing his hands up and down the legs of his pants as if worried at how sweaty they were.

"Wasn't it?" I agreed, but I couldn't quite make my smile work. This was hard. I held out a hand to him. "Come on."

"What? Where?" he stammered.

"Just come with me," I said, thrusting my hand out at him again.

I could see him fighting the urge to argue. I was sure he was going to insist that he didn't dance, or something similar.

But in the end, he slid his hand in mine and let me pull him to his feet. Then I led the way, tugging him along behind me like a toddler who doesn't want to leave the playground yet.

It was only when I came to a stop, not on the dance floor but right before where Jessica was standing chatting with Michelle and Kristofer, that he realized what was happening.

"Ingrid?" he said, and tried to pull his hand out of mine. But I didn't let him go. Not until I had caught Jessica's hand and brought the two of them together.

"There," I said. "That's as it should be."

"Um, Ingrid?" Now it was Michelle saying my name like I had suddenly gone crazy.

"What, you didn't know?" I asked her. Jessica and Andrew were both blushing furiously and very carefully not looking at anyone, certainly not at each other.

But they also weren't letting go of each other's hands.

"Oh," Michelle said, her eyes wide. "Oh, that's what's been going on? I take a semester's worth of classes, and everyone's lives just rocket away when I'm not looking."

"I know, right?" I said. "I'm not sure why anyone felt like anything had to be a *secret*, though. No one here is anything but happy for the two of you."

"Over the moon," Michelle said.

"Really?" Andrew said in total disbelief, and Jessica looked up at me with nervous fear in her eyes.

"Really," I said as firmly as I could. "I wish you would've said something. But I guess you were planning to."

Andrew gave Jessica a questioning glance, and she flushed even deeper as she nodded.

"I've been away, and life moved on," I said. "And it makes total sense. I love you both, and I can see how what I love about both of you just fits together. I'm so happy you're together."

"Well, we're not, actually," Andrew said.

"Happy?"

"Together," he said.

But he clearly wasn't happy either.

"We agreed…" Jessica started, but couldn't quite figure out how to end the sentence.

"But you are as of now?" I said. "Happy and together both?"

They looked at each other, and then they both just started to glow in a way I didn't need magical perceptions to see.

"Right, so off to the dance floor, both of you," I said, making shooing motions with my hands. "And Jessica, don't let him tell you he doesn't dance. He can move his feet while you dance, right?"

"Right!" Jessica agreed, and taking Andrew's hand in both of hers, dragged him towards the dance floor. She looked my way in passing and mouthed a fervent, "Thank you!"

And then they were gone.

"I didn't get any of that," Kristofer said with a chuckle.

"Neither did I," said Thorbjorn, suddenly standing just behind me.

"I'll explain everything," Michelle said to Kristofer, then grinned at me as she dragged him away towards one of the already food-laden tables.

"There was a path to a happy ending with a roadblock in it," I said as I turned to look up at Thorbjorn. "I just had to clear the way."

He looked over at Andrew and Jessica dancing together. Or, rather, Andrew was shuffling his feet more or less to the beat while Jessica danced in circles around him. But they were still both glowing.

"It looks like another wedding is on the way," Thorbjorn said approvingly.

"Well, they might take it a little slower than your brother and Kara did," I said. "But I think eventually they'll get there."

"Everyone has their own pace, I suppose," he said with a twinkle in his eye. Then he bent forward, pulling aside the neck of his tunic to show me his bare shoulder. "Do you see what your cat did to me?"

"Sorry, I know how a cat scratch can burn. But he was just so happy to see me," I said.

"He wasn't the only one," Thorbjorn said, his voice suddenly an intense rumble. "I don't know how you did it."

"What, get back inside? After fixing the mead hall, it wasn't much trouble," I said.

"No, I don't know how you could stand it. When I was trapped in that tower for weeks and weeks and you didn't know where I was or when you'd see me again. I slept through most of that, you know. I didn't even think about what it was like for you," he said. Then he raised an eyebrow, making his statement a question.

"It was hard," I admitted. "Let's not do it again, okay?"

"Not even for three days," he said. "Not without knowing how to find each other again."

"Agreed," I said.

Not that I had any idea how we were going to manage that. Our responsibilities were a lot, and I knew neither one of us was willing to give them up.

But we'd figure something out. Maybe it was the wedding vibes talking, but in the bright light of a Midsummer afternoon, with a rousing song in my ears and the smell of a feast in the making filling the air, everything felt doable.

"Come, Ingrid Torfudottir," Thorbjorn said as he took my hand. "It's my brother's wedding, and we are going to dance till dawn."

That was a plan I could live with.

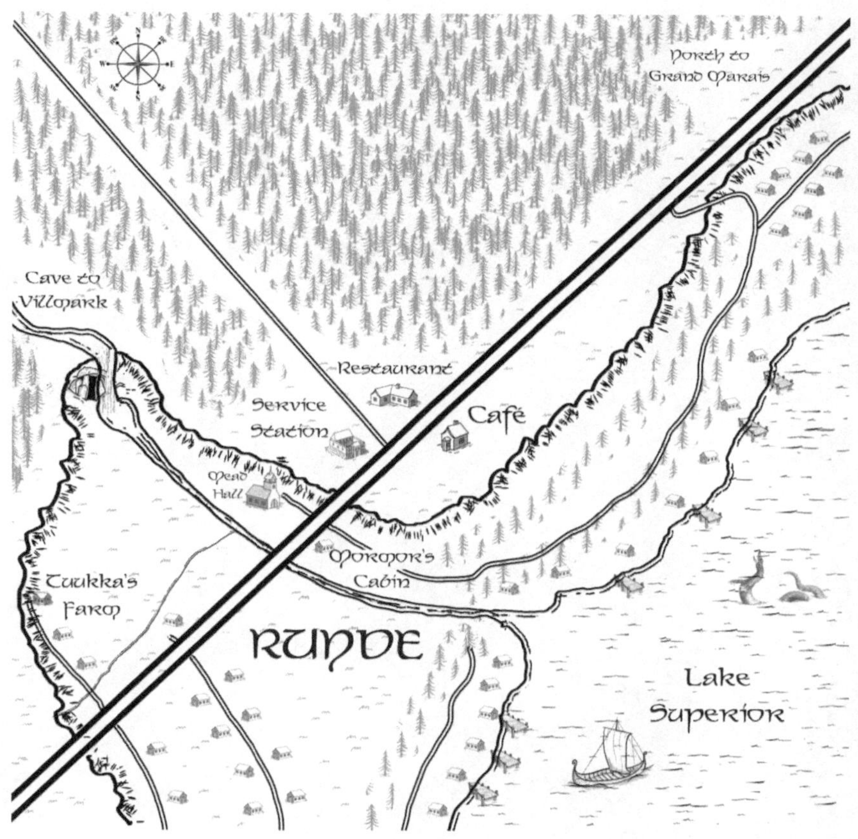

North to
Grand Marais
Cave to
Villmark
Restaurant
Service
Station
Café
Mead
Hall
Mormor's
Cabin
Tuukka's
Farm
RUNDE
Lake
Superior

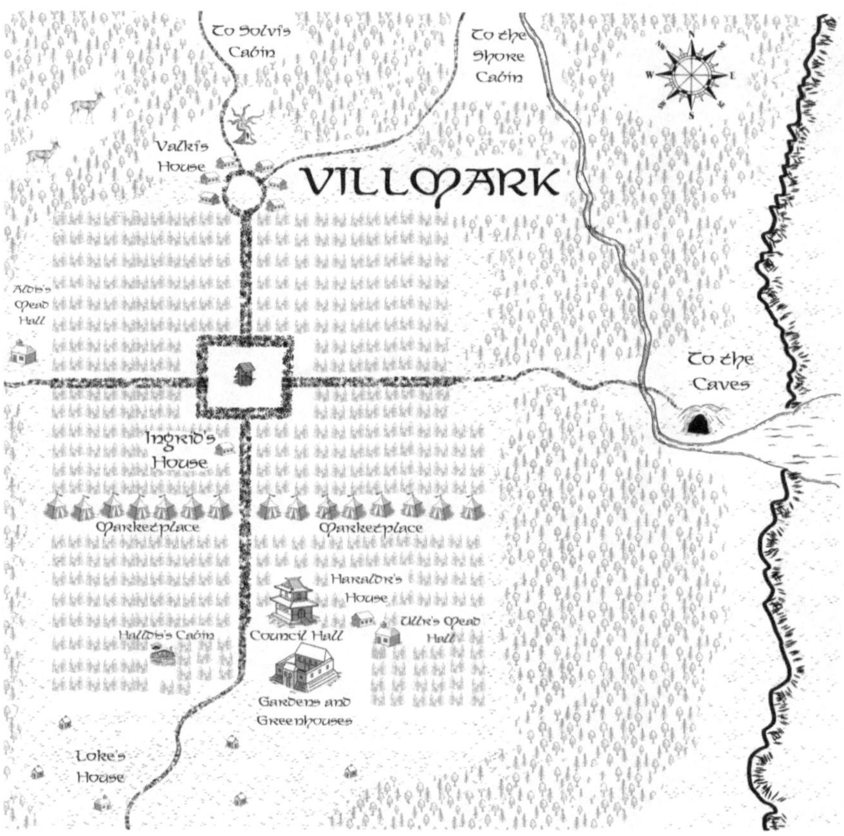

To Solvi's Cabin
To the Shore Cabin
Valki's House
VILLMARK
Aldi's Mead Hall
To the Caves
Ingrid's House
Marketplace
Marketplace
Haraldr's House
Halldis's Cabin
Council Hall
Ullr's Mead Hall
Gardens and Greenhouses
Loke's House
N
S
E
W

CHECK OUT BOOK ELEVEN!

The Viking Witch will return in **Assassination in the Glade**, available now!

Ingrid Torfa lives two lives. In one she struggles to get by as a book illustrator in the tiny town of Runde on the North Shore of Lake Superior in Minnesota.

But in the other, she serves as a Norse witch, a volva, in the town of Villmark, where the descendants of a lost colony of Vikings hides inside a pocket dimension far from the reach of the modern world.

Usually, balancing the needs of those two worlds dominate her time and energy.

But this time, Villmark offers her trouble enough to consume her. Young men keep disappearing in the fields south of Villmark, a place of no danger in the past. The council tells her to leave it to the guardians known as the Thors.

Then one of the Thors turns up with mixed up memories. And a missing brother.

Now not even the council can stop Ingrid from getting to

the bottom of this latest mystery. Because her own Thorbjorn just might be next.

Assassination in the Glade is book 11 in **The Viking Witch Mystery Series!**

THE WITCHES THREE
COZY MYSTERIES

In case you missed it, check out **Charm School**, the first book in the complete **Witches Three Cozy Mystery Series**!

Amanda Clarke thinks of herself as perfectly ordinary in every way. Just a small-town girl who serves breakfast all day in a little diner nestled next to the highway, nothing but dairy farms for miles around. She fits in there.

But then an old woman she never met dies, and Amanda was named in her will. Now Amanda packs a bag and heads to the big city, to Miss Zenobia Weekes' Charm School for Exceptional Young Ladies. And it's not in just any neighborhood. No, she finds herself on Summit Avenue in St. Paul, a street lined with gorgeous old houses, the former homes of lumber barons, railroad millionaires, even the writer F. Scott Fitzgerald. Why, Amanda can practically hear the jazz music still playing across the decades.

Scratch that. The music really, literally, still plays in the backyard of the charm school. Because the house stretches across time itself. Without a witch to protect this tear in the fabric of the world, anything can spill over. Like music.

Or like murder.

Charm School, the first book in the complete **Witches Three Cozy Mystery Series!**

214

THE WEAL & WOE BOOKSHOP
WITCH MYSTERIES

In case you missed it, check out **The Teashop Terror**, the first book in the complete **Weal & Woe Bookshop Witch Mystery Series**!

No one knows more about every branch of magic than Tabitha Greene. She devoted years to studying the most esoteric texts, hunting down the most obscure source materials, and deciphering the most cryptic ancient scrolls. But her career in academia hits a dead end when no wizard will take her on as an apprentice.

Just because, despite being descended from two long and prestigious lines of witches, her attempts to actually perform any magic always fail. Often spectacularly.

But no more college means no more dorm life. And no magical skills means no real job skills, at least, not in the witchy world. And a life spent moving from school to school every few months was a life without real friendships. She finds herself alone with nowhere to go.

Then an uncle she barely remembers offers her a summer job, running his bookstore over the summer. The Weal and Woe Bookstore, located in a magical pocket world within a block of buildings just north of the old Mill District of Minneapolis, Minnesota.

Not exactly the pinnacle of all her hopes and dreams. But it's just for one summer, right?

Or so Tabitha tells herself. But unbeknownst to her, the Weal and Woe Bookstore is about to change her life.

The Teashop Terror, the first book in the complete **Weal & Woe Bookshop Witch Mystery Series**!

and Fitz Sci-Fi Murder Mysteries, available everywhere books are sold.

FREE EBOOK!

Like exclusive, free content?

If you'd like to receive "A Collection of Witchy Prequels", a free collection of short story prequels to the Witches Three Cozy Mystery and Viking Witch Mystery series, as well as other free stories throughout the year, go to my website CateMartin.com to subscribe to my newsletter! This eBook is exclusively for newsletter subscribers and will never be sold in stores. Check it out!

ABOUT THE AUTHOR

Cate Martin has written stories which have appeared in **Mystery, Crime and Mayhem** quarterly magazine as well as in the annual **Holiday Spectacular** Advent calendar of Christmas stories. She is also the author of three witch mystery series: **The Witches Three Cozy Mysteries**, and **The Viking Witch Mysteries** and **The Weal and Woe Bookshop Witch Mysteries**. She currently lives in Minneapolis, Minnesota. You can learn more about her work at CateMartin.com.

Ashes Beneath the Tree (available July 14, 2026 direct from me or August 11, 2026 in stores everywhere)

The Viking Witch Mysteries Books 1-3

The Viking Witch Mysteries Books 4-6

The Viking Witch Mysteries Books 7-9

The Weal & Woe Bookshop Witch Mystery Series

The Teashop Terror

The Salon & Spa Scandal

The Bookseller Blunder

The Entrepreneur Enigma

The Novelty Shop Nightmare

The Courtyard Conundrum

Short Story Collections

Bubbly, Bicycles and Brides

The Dorothy Lundegaard Mysteries

Fruitcake, Festivities and Firelight